Swimming from the Flames

Swimming from the Flames

Stories by
Pauline Holdstock

Turnstone Press

Copyright © 1995 Pauline Holdstock

Turnstone Press
607-100 Arthur Street
Winnipeg, Manitoba
Canada   R3B 1H3

All rights reserved. No part of this book may be reproduced or transmitted in any form or by any means—graphic, electronic or mechanical—without the prior written permission of the publisher. Any request to photocopy any part of this book shall be directed in writing to the Canadian Copyright Licensing Agency.

Turnstone Press gratefully acknowledges the assistance of the Canada Council and the Manitoba Arts Council.

Some of these stories have appeared in *The Antigonish Review, Event, Exile, Grain, The Malahat Review, The New Quarterly, NeWest Review, Pierian Spring, This Magazine, Waves,* and the anthology *True North/Down Under.*

Cover art: Kerri Andrews

Author photo: John Holdstock

Design: Manuela Dias

This book was printed and bound in Canada by Hignell Printing for Turnstone Press.

Canadian Cataloguing in Publication Data

Holdstock, Pauline
Swimming from the flames
Fiction.
ISBN 0-88801-182-2
I. Title
PS8565.O622S8 1995   C813'.54   C94-920249-5
PR9199.3.H662S8 1995

For Jess, Silas, Leo, and Sophie

and in memory of my father

Acknowledgments

The author would like to thank the editors of the magazines where some of these stories first appeared. She is especially grateful for the early support of the late Brenda Riches.

Special thanks also to John for time to write and to M.A.C. Farrant for good advice on everything . . .

CONTENTS

The Swimming Story 1

Lost And Found 7

At Sea in the Wood 17

Secluded Setting, Close Beach 25

The Devil and the Deep 31

Blind Spot 39

Bloody Dog 47

The Turn of the Year 55

Not at This Address 67

Memento 77

Hagar 83

Fairy Tale 87

Samson's Wife 93

Only Yesterday 99

Sitting Pretty 107

Faces 113

Burning Bright 123

THE SWIMMING STORY

LUCIA'S MOTHER WAS BORN IN A SUN-BLEACHED VILLAGE on the shores of the Adriatic where she ran barefoot through her brown-limbed childhood.
    That's a beginning. Whether or not one can swallow sun-bleached villages and brown-limbed childhood whole, it's a beginning. Lucia's mother went on, when she was a slight seventeen, to swim an icy lake somewhere in the Apennines. It was wartime and she carried a message to allied troops on the other side of the pass. Like a Hollywood German Shepherd.
    The story has a middle where Lucia's mother is old and fat and boring and lives in Toronto. She never speaks about her brave and sunny past. The middle is promisingly depressing.
    But it has an end too. Lucia sees her old, fat, boring mother swim Beaver Lake and she's filled with admiration. Among other things.
    Beginning-middle-end stories, however, are not the thing. Lucia's mother, then, must windmill indefinitely through Canadian, through Italian, waters, head down, alone, without witness, without acclaim.

The Swimming Story

Brava, Mama! Brava!

I could tell about another mother. This one also old but not without rebellion. A diehard. She learns to paint in oils, to live without makeup or permanents, to get political, to love another woman's children, to read Garcia Marquez, to eat calamari, miso, matzo, antipasto, tofu, dim sum, imam bayaldi . . . She would eat the earth if only it would not eat her.

Now she learns to swim, forcing her arthritic neck down to dip her face in the turquoise chlorine. But it's my mother and it's not fiction, it's cheating. Nevertheless, it must be said, her shoulders speak. Thick, rounded, unjointed, they bow over the surface of the chest-high water. All around her, other shoulders dip and bob, come up glistening, smooth blades, plates of bone sliding easily beneath brown skin. Only the mother's, my mother's, shoulders remain bowed, solid, while her throat bursts with the word "Swim!" and her eyes burn with chlorine, or the effort, or perhaps with a memory imagined.

It's hard, of course, not to cheat since life is packed tight with stories. It's hard not to touch them.

This one. A young boy. He's a lad, a loon, a light in his parents' eyes. He makes them laugh. He teaches himself to play the violin. He makes them cry. To join the navy he lies about his age and then he writes his parents friendly, happy letters and signs them, "All for now," "All the best, Dad. Look after Mum," and "All love." But it's wartime and before long his ship is blown apart.

The parents cry a lot. The mother takes the longest journey of her aproned life to Whitehall to find his name officially.

The boy's name, even with the others, does not help.

Some months later, the brass knocker clatters at the green front door of the terraced house and the boy's mother, drying her hands on a floral pinny, opens her nicely papered hallway to a tidal wave of freezing North Sea darkness. The boy (another boy) has come, he says, to tell her how it was. Thought she might like to know how Jack finished.

So she sits, and the awkward shipmate fills her parlour with sudden death: explosions in the hold, shattered bulkheads, and cold, cold water under a spreading skin of spilled oil. And then the oil is alight and there is no helping anyone in the panic, though he does look.

The boy, the friend, then tells his own swimming story and the mother cries with happiness when he reaches a lifeboat. He leaves her with a teacup in her hand and treads with care across the lino in the hall.

Kind as he is though, he has to tell it all and before he leaves he whispers to the sister. No, nothing. Nothing he could do. Last he saw when he turned to look, Jack's head, above the waves, was all alight. He went down burning. The sister keeps the secret for one year before she tells the mother. The mother lives for forty-five more years with the image of her son's head, alight, above the water.

But this again is trickery and will never do. This story has been lived. No need to write it. No need to prompt sympathy, empathy, anguish. This has been done. And anyway it, too, had an ending. And a bitter coda.

So I sit (and it is within sound of the small rush of each wave) and I search for a story that is not quite true, that is at least embroidered, and one that has maybe a beginning, maybe a middle or an end, but God forbid all three.

There's this. A marathon swimmer. A hearty, gritty woman, an ageless schoolgirl cased in blubber, thrashing her way across Lake Superior, the English Channel. She has had few friends, few and moderate, always moderate, successes and very predictable failures. The swim is her bid for magnificence.

I swim to find out what happens to her. The water slips apart, lips over my shoulders, slides away. My hands dip and cut, pull and feather. The water curtains down from my, her, raised arm. She sees none of it. Her head is down. Her face turns only at intervals and then hardly at all, an eighth of a turn at most, enough only to let her mouth suck in the hollow of air behind the pillowed wave. A blind gulp in the cold.

The Swimming Story

And the idea of the story comes like a bubble, intact, rolling on the surface of the water. This woman's determination, like an Edwardian bathing dress, is more comic than splendid. And she knows it. The knowledge lends only greater urgency to every stroke.

She swims faster. Her body remembers how to ride the buffetings so that the punching waves no longer stop it dead but lift it. Her body listens to the rhythms, sings with them. Epiphany. It's all there is and all that is necessary. Zen Buddhism in the Straits of Juan de Fuca.

All there is? A seeping away of human consciousness into a transcendental sea? There's more, surely, than that, than the endless, numbing dip-pull, dip-pull over the quick rhythm of the interminably fluttering feet. There's failure. Or even death. There's always *something*.

And yet the image of the swimmer sticks, like sand on my damp towel. The body slipping through fluent space, head down, cutting through a surface blotted with cloud, splashed with sun. The body spiralled in green light, green shadows, in the ubiquitous touch, no touch, of water. There is that. And a fish-eye view of an angled arm and droplets spangling down, the palm a blade, cutting in, the arms a windmill, milling the slow water, finding the torque that propels the body on through, rolling for the next breath.

That again is a start but it goes nowhere, only on through the changing, the unchanging, the liquid light. There is no story. There is only the cool sheen where the bubble rolled.

Is that then all my preoccupation? A concern not with the action, the event, but with the essential medium? Water as life. Water whence we all crawled in our fishier days, in our dark and slimy past. Water the solution, the amniotic fluid of the earth. It came as a surprise to find the fallopian waters brine, the ova washed to their womb/ocean on salty tides. And then it was no surprise.

But the fictions, the swimming stories, are fictions—or facts—of death. The end is always death. Fear of death, knowledge of death are all the middle. The beginning is nothing but a premonition.

But we want no premonitions. We want no premonitions, no coincidences and no nasty turns. These are a mockery of life.

And yet.

Life is tightly mazed with these, with nasty turns and all the rest. It is a booby-trapped labyrinth.

Swimming as escape perhaps? Fleeing the enemy machine guns, the advance of old age, the clutches of a cold vertical mile of water. Swimming from the flames.

But it doesn't feel like escape. It feels like a homecoming, a re-entry. The water encircles, enfolds, embraces, envelops. The blood calls. Tide within a tide. The limbs soften, flow into liquid space. Eyes dissolve in light. The feet, a fishtail, vibrate to the rhythms of creation. It is a return to the elemental broth, the universal stew.

Is it simple, then, like that? The source of life, the womb, the journey back? There's one more story I'm failing still to tell.

A young woman. Her face worn out with smoking, with drinking, with fighting back. Every last thing she never wanted has been thrown her way. (Life a bully coach, relentless."Here, catch! Take it, take it! *Hang* in there! *Hang* in!")

It starts with motherhood in grade eleven and gets worse: jailed husband, drunken lovers, dead friends. The list is variable. There can be an idiot baby that she loves but it dies anyway.

She's wiry though and tough. She won't let go, won't let the team down. Would never think to hurt any of her own side—idiots especially, but moral destitutes as well.

Coach is a bastard."One more," he says. "Brain tumour. Got it? *Hang on!*"

Enough, she says. She checks the freezer. She tidies her room. She puts on a bathing suit under pale jeans and a grubby sweater. Picking up a towel, she remembers with embarrassment that she won't need one. Decides even so to leave it on the beach where she often swims when she's had enough. This detail pleases her since it is not her intention to hurt anyone.

She waits until dark.

At the water's edge she walks in steadily, evenly. There seems to be no point in flinching or shivering. Only when the mass of water will not take another stride does she tilt forward and give her shoulders, her throat, her face to the cold black light.

An obvious place to end. But for her it's not so easy. She swims out. She swims for more than twice the time it takes to kill a man in water this cold. She swims past the place where she had planned to stop.

And now she is crying. She doesn't want to wash up where the children might get to know or see. So although she has lost all feeling in her feet, and her arms feel like inflated rubber limbs, barely able to move, she swims.

She gulps the salty, brown-tasting water, her face, her ears numb, disappeared already, a pain left in their place. And still the water hasn't pulled her down into its warmer depths. Her arms move scarcely at all.

"Now!" she says but when she tries to stop, her limbs jerk alive, resist the pull, keep her afloat.

Float.

She looks around her. The water is polished with moonlight, its small waves shining like cut coal. She rolls on her back, and her eyes, though they are scorched with tears, see the black sky spattered with stars. She closes them inside her head. Her legs, though she cannot feel them, kick gently. The water, a black silk canopy, arches beneath her and she is weightless, numb.

This an ocean/womb, an elemental broth? No, this ocean is death. It's what she wants, what she has spent her life swimming for, to. A solution. To dissolve the pain.

The numbed body rolls from the canopy, drifts under it, weightless. No sound. Liquid light become liquid darkness. Silky night. No waves. No resistance. The mouth, filled with salt tears, opens, spills them.

LOST AND FOUND

FIRST WOMAN

Losing Control

Control was what she lost most frequently but—she always the speedway queen—never quite.

From her earliest years she practised the tantrum, biting the hands that fed her, throwing peas and carrots with skill at walls, bruising the ground with her fists. Even then she was fast, could take herself on short legs to the very edge, and there, adroit, sidestep, smile and watch the others, who in consternation followed, hurtle over. Teachers parents friends and sisters always fell for it. Or over it.

And later lovers. Tantrums now exquisite. Tantric. Control absolute. For all the while hurling shoes and makeup, pacing, pounding, grabbing fistfuls of air, or sometimes hair—and not always her own—and in a frenzy tearing it to shreds, she was conscious of her staging, mindful of her choreography, breaking glass never by accident and not once taking her eyes from the eyes that watched her as she drove them, goatish, into a deeper dark.

Coming down was heaven: the slow involuntary—so she

would have them seem—waves of indignation that beat back and forth slower, slower across the room, across the protagonists, until they lay, flayed, raw, every word a hurt, every hurt tasted. She loved it. Though her lovers as a rule did not and would leave, but only after they had given what she wanted, thought she needed.

Finding a Husband / Crock of Gold
There was a man who happened by, quiet and gentle, with several bank accounts and all of them stuffed to bursting with wads of dollar bills. He had a strong conviction that his money was a sexual attraction. She, on the other hand, liked the way he knew her game but would not play it, loped easy in soft shoes away from the edge. And, too, she was partial to his knees, capped as they were with square plates of bone of improbably sharp definition. The rest of him beneath the dark wool suit was not a disappointment. Marrying this body that she wanted, thought she needed, was easy, not to say expected at the time. And all his worldly goods.

The toys, the red TR6, the skis and tennis rackets, the thick white towels, these were a distraction but not for long, unresponsive as they were. And then the man had a certain solidity about him despite his loping style. Time and again she showed him the edge, offered to go over with him but he refused to take the leap, would rather slide into a pinstripe and sidle off to close a few more deals.

Her need to engage another soul was as unremitting as the need to bite.

Losing Her Hold
He wanted babies and obligingly she had a daughter but it was enough. She had not expected to be asked to give so much, and all at once. This child was too like herself. Eager to play on the precarious cliff-top and sure-footed, she could run on thin legs to the brink, the mother snatching at her hair behind. And the mother, though she could see where she was being led, was always left scrabbling. She

would have liked not to play again, but the child knew how with a word, a look, to drive her.

And yet she loved her daughter, within reason, respected her more than anything for her courage in the game, honoured her for the humbling knowledge that she taught.

Now more than ever, seeing the man's attempts to hide his disappointment in this daughter who was not at all the family he intended, she felt compelled to please him. Who continued to be kind, and generous. To this end when her self surfaced inopportunely she would shove it down, hold its head under until the bubbles were no longer noticeable. After a while she was able to watch its frequent drownings without submitting to the urge to scream.

Losing Her Head

Only once did she lose her head. And her heart with it. And all her strong-arm tactics were insufficient. The man was very beautiful, smooth-skinned, young. For him she shook out the spangles of the speedway queen again, gaudy and fast, but hardly dared to put them on. To lie with him she left the daughter, listless by the pool, and drove away. It was summer and as she drove her eyes would almost close against the glare, the need.

She had a tape that he made for her, his own voice fluid and dark, even on the filmy ribbon. So she would drive, the windows open, the words streaming past her from the dash, over her eyes, her lips, over her cheeks, words combing her hair, slipping into her ears, her mouth, drowning her, until she stood before him in the slatted shadow of his room, her clothes around her feet.

It should have been enough but always she told herself there was something more, and one day, just to see, she put on the gaudy costume, revved her emotional machine and took him for a spin, unsticking the ground beneath them. He at first held tight to her, angry, but then seeing the brink loom, let go and alone she plunged over.

Losing Her Husband

Strangely, she did not. Perhaps he did not find the tape to which she drove. Or did. Perhaps there was nothing for her to lose. He was a busy man and spent much time away deciding what to buy, what sell. At home it was his custom to adress her only rarely, not wishing to provoke a scene which, he had learned, she could conjure out of nothing. His absence, like his presence, was neither here nor there.

Losing Her Mind

Losing her mind was not a process but an occurrence. Like losing a hat in a high wind. Watching her lover watching her fall she felt it go, sucked away by the speed of her descent.

Left with the lump of knowledge that she had snatched on the way down, she took to lying long hours in bed to ponder it: the incontrovertible fact of her aloneness. She lost whole days. They drained away like tepid bath water while she languished uneasily. Dinner was an afterthought, a hit and miss affair. At table she would watch her husband and her daughter working the strings of meat around their mouths. She knew what they were thinking and said it first: *You've lost all sense of proportion, get your priorities right.* What did they want for heaven's sake? A hot meal every night? They ate in silence.

She began to read. She rifled books for the clues they might surrender and found everywhere evidence of isolation. Her husband told her she was losing her sense of direction. She should take up evening classes.

Her loneliness now tremendous, she went to church. Then she was hopeful and, facing the heavy oak door, held her breath. Waiting for the Spirit. Inside, however, there were people—those she had failed to anticipate—corralled, far from any edge, knowing what to say, what do, their voices and their bodies rising and falling in unison.

To circumvent this community of souls she went alone to the priest, lacking the courage for God. The priest sighed, put on a piece of purple silk over his rugby shirt and heard her Confession there in his office. Rain dripped off the cedar outside the window, and a voice from the TV in the living room assured them both that Coke was It.

Finding Her Feet Again

In time she grew to accept the knowledge that had once so alarmed. She looked at her husband, who seemed not to mind at all (though surely he knew, she being the last, it was clear, to find out the fact of life), and she looked at her daughter, who grew, and raged, but would survive. People did survive, having no option. The days themselves were some use. The routine of them, the sameness was a comfort; it was the trapeze to which she clung, from which she took flight, to which she clung. It might have been perpetual motion, had she not known. And yet, as before, the flight, the fright, was everything. Sometimes she took a chance, hung in mid-air at full stretch, spangled legs helpless behind her, palms and fingers hooking air in front. But she would be lucky, the bar returning, striking with a shock, snatching her up, back to the small platform where there was only room for one.

SECOND WOMAN

Finding Time

There were so many babies. Finding the time did become a problem. And the room. It did not help at all to know that time and space were curved. She tried not to plot her days like positions on a graph. Nothing was more linear than her own time; it was a track, and the space she wanted to reach was an empty room upon it, a cube that, strangely, diminished at her approach, so that she managed to slip in only briefly before emerging on the other side. Often, just as she was about to step inside, the babies themselves would be there. Ma, ma, ma. Needing. Kneading her heart into pulp until she had to tear it out, scoop it out for them, doling: Here, and here. Take, take. Scooping and hollowing her self out, eyes on the narrow door. Let me go. Until she would step over the wiggling babies, still needing, wanting more, and close the door.

Still they would be there when she came out the other side. Her babies happy now, no longer needing, forcing her with their oblivion to bend to them (I'm here, let me come back), lacing their lives to hers with their nonchalance.

It was not that she did not enjoy her life on the track, but inside the cube, space was cornered, time suspended and everything was possible—even falling off the track, which could be dreamed here in immunity, no repercussions ever.

But there was another danger. She might emerge incomplete, part of her still inside the cube. Then her hands would muddle at the soup, the shoelaces, her ears open to receive the plaints and whimpers, the needings when they began again, her eyes fixed and distant while she tried to remember what it was she had lost.

Losing Her Husband

Losing her husband was a blessing, she decided, and not only in defence. She had found it difficult, folding up her self each morning, tucking it under the pillow. It had been tedious, dressing its empty body in the clothes her husband bought her, ones with labels, going hatted and heeled, into the world, a real wife.

To begin with she had performed this act often and happily, liking to see her husband's pleasure, but as time wore on she grew less conscientious in the task, or bored.

She would appear at dinner with the dirt from the potato planting grimed deep into the cracks in her fingers; in her teeth, it might have been, for all the polite conversation she could make. In time she was called upon to effect her transformation less and less frequently until her husband saw that she brought him no advantage in the world and that it might be more expedient to keep her to the house, saving weddings or funerals.

He stayed on for a while, returning each day from his glass tower to suffer the mess of babies, emptying his pockets into their fat hands. The babies were voracious. They opened their red throats to receive entire rivers of milk and grain, stretched their mouths around truckloads of shoes and shirts and dental bills. At last he found it less trying to mail a cheque. From some distance. It was a relief. And not only for him.

Losing Heart

Not *her* heart, you understand, but heart. Sometimes she would rise to a day rare and shining and see too clearly its place upon the graph, a small square, thirty-eight large squares along, an indeterminate number (she would not guess) from the edge. Then she would want to take it and make of it something wonderful, a keepsake in silver, exquisite, intricate and polished, but there would be a baby crying and porridge burning and all the small shoes not cleaned and the phone ringing and the cat walking by with a bird and it still flapping. . . . dear God! The shining day all trampled, muddied somewhere underneath the torn ski-jacket and the spilled box of Cheerios out in the hall, while she and the boy shed tears for the bird they thought they had saved (in a box of wood shavings) suddenly dead, its heart sticking out of it like a pebble.

Finding a Purpose

Though her friends and family urged her to try it, like a new evening class, or a fitness regime, finding a purpose was not a pursuit she had ever cared for. She was raising children, stacking them up, backup copies, against the inevitable. Merely living, she held, was quite enough, considering the alternative, and since her earliest days she had not ceased to consider. Besides, there was barely time to live at all. So much servicing a family needed, and a house.

Friends said it was no kind of life, flicked their white towels over their shoulders and took themselves off to the beach, the club. She was missing her best years, she was a fool. Until her husband left, and then she was a victim and they, not foreseeing the lover and his money and his taste in pregnant women, rather liked her for it.

There were rewards. To take the babies out at noon, fed or not, for air, watch them gulp it down so full of ozone it fizzed in their throats. To suffocate in their soft hair. It was enough.

Finding Herself Pregnant Again

Loaded with its sense of passive accident, the phrase perfectly suited her repetitious discovery, for, after the first, she never could find it in her heart to preconceive her babies, though she did need them.

At the first birth, the old woman from the corner farm had come to call. Hobbling through the stubble of her life, distrustful of the strangers who were her neighbours, she had come nevertheless with a gift, its ribbon stuck through with a sprig of white plum. Her hands were large, the joints all thickened and no more use, the skin loose where the flesh had gone, and waxy. She put her palm on the baby's head. "There," she said. "If you knew. If you only knew." The words came as no surprise to the mother, who, while the child was still slippery from the birth, had seen her own blood upon its head and had wanted to apologize.

Yet still each time she let it happen and when the lover in the dark suit soft-shoed it to the scene, barefooted it into her bed, she let it happen all over again, knowing she had never in any case been able to get enough of this confirmation, affirmation, this life-in-the-face-of-death business, this wildest thrill of all.

To perform the stunt so dangerously close to the edge was exhilaration of a kind of which she would never tire. To see life turn at the last, the first, moment and clutch at the wind-blown grass with star-shaped hands, feet perfect like little fish flying above the dark and eyes amazed and looking. For her. This was living.

It left her friends with a whole new set of things to say. Hadn't she had enough of that? Hadn't she heard of the pill, for God's sake? Her smile was irritating. Didn't she miss it? What? Everything. No she didn't miss anything at all. Never felt more fulfilled. Fuller, she would say, waving to them as they climbed into their yellow jeeps, their black Suzukis and headed for the mountains. She would go then with her pleasant rolling walk down to the warm lake, shamble in, belly first and wallow there, buoyed by the knowledge that her lover was rich enough to allow her thus to indulge the habit they seemed to share.

Finding Herself Alone
The friends tired of her fleshiness and her milky smile. They left her to the bed that she had made. The lover would have joined her there, so little comfort did he find in the dry elegance of his own house. He had a wife, he complained, a consort really, a mere escort who looked good upon his arm. He would have liked a family. His wife's selfishness was without bounds, he said. The taut silk of this woman's belly, her heavy breasts. His teeth ached for the taste of milk. Yes he would have joined her there, had it been more convenient financially.

And had she wanted him. Bearing children was such a personal affair.

It did not do at all to have an extraneous lover clothing her in motherhood; it was just another costume with a label and she was ill-suited for the role. She bore children more for the secrets that they promised to reveal than for any blind dependence. She watched the children, intent at play, hood their eyes against her laser gaze, hide what shone there under the lashes. Misers with liquid silver, letting fall only a drop each day to roll into her cupped palm. And why should they give her more? The track, from where they stood, was endless.

But the children grew. Some left to seek their fathers, interesting as those figures had become by removing from the scene. The rest simply left. Some took colourful excursions to foreign lands where they conducted exotic interludes. Others spun out of control for a brief and heady season. But all of them began, sooner or later, to find their way about the world, in a way she never had. They began to talk of rewarding positions of exciting challenge and nice pieces of property. She dyed her hair orange and took to wearing second-hand silk, for its colours and even when it frayed, the threads wafting like fine hair through the house. Like her days. They passed her now almost without touching, so intent she was upon the earth, digging and hoeing, jabbing life into it and pulling it out by the roots. How she hated to be found at it by her children, who did not understand, who no longer seemed to have silver enough even for themselves but had to ask their silly questions. What are you planting? As if she were a fisherman: Have you caught anything?

Better they should find her swimming naked in the lake—let them think of some new questions—or lying in bed at three, ravelled in days real and imagined, unmindful of imminent endings, time no longer a track. And often they did. Or she would go in work-boots up onto the roof to clear the leaves. From her vantage point she could see them more clearly as they sprang out of their TR6s, white towels waving. Up there in the risky blue, she could be glad that they were happy. Or anyway smiling.

AT SEA IN THE WOOD

"YOU'RE ON A PATH THROUGH THESE WOODS," RODDIE IS saying. His face is round and eager, leaning close to Jane's.

Jane, always easily intrigued, nods, keen as a Girl Guide. Derek rustles his *Globe & Mail.* Jane has an enthusiasm for games; it irks him.

"So you're on this path," prompts Roddie.

"Yes, I'm on this path," Jane closes her eyes, concentrating.

"And—?"

"It's dark. Dark and winding," she says. Roddie beams his thick lenses, knowingly, over at Derek. Derek shakes out his paper and begins to fold it with meticulous attention to the edges.

"And it's, it's—"

"Overgrown?" suggests Roddie.

"Oh, yes. It's very overgrown. Entangled. It's full of roots and things that tend to trip you up."

"And there's a mountain in front of you."

"All right," agrees Jane, although it doesn't really seem to belong. "A sort of rocky cliff face." Roddie hugs his knees and grins in absurd delight from Jane to Derek and back again.

"And now you come to a bridge."

Derek gets up to leave. Jane has trouble managing the bridge. She wants to say that it is massy grey stone, humpbacked and solid, but when she begins to speak the bridge sways and flattens out to a wooden structure, nothing but a few slippery boards laid down across a body of bottle-green water. It is more a path than a bridge and Jane is on it, its fixed end somewhere behind her. The rest snakes out in front. It is not wide enough for two people to pass. It floats on the back of the water and stretches away like a railroad track across a dark prairie. There are no handrails at the side, only the short boards laid like sleepers underfoot, slack on the surface of the water. It undulates. There is no question but that Jane must walk this floating bridge, no question at all. There is no other possibility. It sways so much that Jane gets down on hands and knees to crawl it. And then this pontoon stops abruptly in the middle of the open sea, its unfinished end floating free, going nowhere.

"Hm," says Roddie. "Hm, O.K. Well let's say you're over the bridge now and there's another path leading away."

Jane looks at her watch. She is late for Morphology at one-thirty. "O.K.," she says, hurriedly closing her eyes. "It's a long one and goes straight up. Now hurry up. I have to go."

"Well then you see a house."

"No I don't. There's nothing there."

"No, you have to. You have to see a house."

"Why?"

"The house is life after death."

"Oh," says Jane.

Cool, efficient, Derek stirs the scrambled eggs.

"How you can be taken in," he says, "by such puerile exercises in that kind of crass pseudo-psychology," he adds two drops of Tabasco, "is beyond me. The Path of Life: mountain equals self-discovery; bridge equals death. You know, don't you," he pauses while he gives three turns to the pepper mill, "you know it shows a distinct immaturity on your part."

Jane wishes he would burn the eggs.

"It's a game," she says, "for heaven's sake."

"You're taking it very seriously—for a game."

"Well it also happens to work. No one tells you to start with why you're being asked these questions but everyone, *everyone* ends up with a projection of their own personal philosophy."

"Plates, please," says Derek.

"It worked on you, didn't it? You had a concrete path. And don't pretend you were just playing us along when you said it. A concrete path! In the woods!"

Derek doesn't answer.

"And a mansion in the mountains!"

The eggs are perfect.

Jane doesn't give up the game. She tries it on most of her friends. Their mountains impress her.

Self-discovery seems to have a lot to do with sex, and it does not surprise her that her friends' mountains are always extravagent and not infrequently exotic; there is even a Vesuvius.

And then there are the bridges. Most people know what they want in a bridge: silver cables suspended over a ravine, a lacquered ebony affair spanning a still pool. Jane would like a good bridge but she doesn't worry about it too much. And she cannot think about the house at all.

The more she reads, the more it seems that it must be the bridges and not the mountains that lead to all the answers. Jane is only trying to find a way out of the wood but people she reads about are always on the lookout for a bridge, are so eager to cross one that they sometimes construct their own.

A bridge implies a purpose; there must be another side to reach—just as there must be a house. One crosses a bridge with the same perfect logic as the chicken crossing the road, Jane supposes. Her own manoeuvres through the wood, however, owe more to the contingencies of evasion than to design, so littered are the paths with roots and rabbit holes and the occasional trap-door.

The trap-doors remind Jane of the penny amusement machines of her childhood, great glass boxes with mechanical figures that clicked and whirred into life when she fed them a coin. She used to watch, mesmerized, as the figures batted through swing doors, fell into coffins and popped out of closets with a cheery, red-nosed disregard of logic.

Jane no longer finds them unlifelike. They would be right at home in her own personal wood. Her father had been the first to disappear. On her twelfth birthday he had fallen, as if struck on the head, at the precise moment that he was stepping into the rowboat to take Jane out on the lake. After the funeral, Jane's mother ran off with a local shopkeeper who, it seemed, had been waiting in the wings all the while. Later there was a friend, Louisa, who embraced leukemia and died angrily, and another, Jenny, who tried with precipitate passion to embrace Jane.

Jane has put her faith in men and is rewarded for this by foul-breathed gropings from her Middle English tutor. She turns to Derek for protection and it is not long before she sprouts a daughter—nor long again before Derek sprints away on his concrete path to the mansion in the mountains, arranging to send her monthly payments along the route.

It seems to Jane that these spots of experience in her life are not connected on any map but stand out like rocks in a choppy sea. Flung upon them, sometimes she clings, sometimes is washed away. And sometimes, when she reaches one and holds on to catch her breath, she can feel it shudder and rumble ominously and she knows nothing is what it seems.

The day she is told formally what she had always known—that she was indeed floundering—was a good day for Jane.

"A2," the doctor says. She takes her pen between thumb and forefinger of both hands, puts it down as if it is a little rod of dynamite, and says, "A2."

Jane is baffled but not alarmed. The examination is a mere formality, a prerequisite for her first job.

The doctor rolls the little stick of dynamite a revolution or two towards Jane and adds that she has grave doubts about signing the certificate of health. Jane suspects that she has been unwise to tell the doctor how often she is beginning to think about the bridge and the house. The doctor clearly considers Jane's myopia to be the least of her problems.

"Psychologically insecure," she says, "with a potentially unstable personality and," as if prompted by the perfidious Derek, "a marked emotional immaturity." The doctor, Jane realizes just as the relevance of the term 'A1' begins to dawn on her, is strongly suggesting that 'A2' was more than she deserves.

Jane is disconcerted and annoyed. For a doctor to behave in this manner with a patient is, she feels, akin to a worker in a food packing plant running amok with the labels. A perfectly ordinary can of beans could come out as 'Mango Chutney,' or 'Pickled Walnuts'.

Chagrined, Jane repeats her story to one or two friends. They respond with a conspicuous lack of concern. "Oh, yes," they say, "that sounds like you." The doctor's description, everyone agrees, was apt—out of line perhaps but apt. Dead on. And they go on to talk about more pressing matters.

To Jane's damaged confidence this lack of concern is balm indeed. It was acceptable, after all, to be living in a sea—never mind that it is in the middle of a wood—in a sea of illogic, chopped by emotional squalls. Her friends themselves are almost at home there.

After this, paths are irrelevant, with or without bridges; Jane accepts the fact that there are only random stepping stones, sometimes only the bare backs of crocodiles. She can survive, she realizes hopping from rock to rock, from back to back. She occasionally even meets other people hopping in the same direction.

Now Jane is at the stove, stirring. Unlike the Derek of a few years ago she does this with no show of expertise or even interest but with a tranquil absent-mindedness. Her daughter, Annie, sits beside her, silent, intent, absorbed in pans and playdough on the floor.

"Mama? Is there any other ways you get dead?"

This is the most ominous arrangement of words Jane has ever heard. A door clicks open in her mind and a chill wind blows across her neck and shoulders. She carries on stirring.

"What do you mean, love?"

"Is there any *other* ways? If you don't have a accident, I mean."

This is exactly what Jane thought she meant. The chill wind enters her blood and runs there like a cold current in a summer sea.

"Well—" Jane stirs now in slow motion and sees every particle of meat, every fleck of pepper, every speck of spice in the pan. "Well, yes. When people get very, very—" on the fast lane in her mind she wonders what Annie's perception of age is and adds two more for safety, "—very, *very* old, then they die."

She feels now as if she might blush before her daughter, as if she has just exposed an obscenity for which she is responsible. She cannot look away from the stove to see her face. There is a thin silence behind her as if Annie has disappeared. Then she hears her daughter's voice again:

"No," Annie says. She adds a little play laugh, especially for Jane. "No, not really. You're tricking me," and she gives the little laugh again the way one might, cornered, throw a trinket in front of an advancing bear.

In the presence of her bravery Jane now must find the courage to witness this her daughter's last stand against the truth.

She turns. The child's vulnerability is like nakedness in snow. Jane longs to cover her but cannot.

"No, love. I'm not tricking you."

She cannot bear to see her daughter staring in disbelief at the truncated end of the floating bridge.

She tries to remember everything she once understood about heaven. She would like to finish building the bridge, erect a ramp, send a vaulting structure soaring to The Other Side, or if not that then at least cobble a handrail where one might wait with dignity.

She loves the child too much to lie.

"Ah, love," she says, and leaves the pan to burn on the stove.

SECLUDED SETTING, CLOSE BEACH

IT SMELLS. IT'S DANK AND DRAB AND IT SMELLS OF MILDEW and mice with a thick overlay of Heaven Scent. Or perhaps it's Raid.
    There's a grubby, gold off-cut put down for summer visitors. Thin nylon sheets cover the fold-away beds. The porch faces north and I know already that I won't want to sit there under the corrugated fibreglass roof where a torn piece of plastic fish-print shower curtain hangs inexplicably from the corner.
    We came for the beach. I want to be down there with the water, the smell of salt and the crab shells. But the others are happy. And Paddy is happiest of all. Look at him. Playing the drunken Irishman: "*Mair*vellous. *Mair*vellous." Prising open beers, handing them round: "This is the place to be. Come on over here." And he hasn't looked outside yet. Walked straight in with his two cases of homemade pale. Celebrating our arrival at this disfigured, slashed open scrape of land that someone has (jokingly, surely) called Arbutus Grove Resort.

The pine needles under my feet are a thousand, a million years deep. They smell of death but they are soft and warm. Here, where the trees begin to thin, harsh grass, fine and spiky, tufts through. A narrow band of sparse, salt-whipped green to cross and then the basalt, moss-covered. The rocks slope, a tilted mass of warm stone, down to the pebbles of the beach. The shoreline curves away north in a fluted oyster shell of rock that disappears in the blue mountainous mist; south, it rises to an outcrop where the great, shaggy arbutus trees loom, like scruffy clouds, to overhang the beach. At the water's edge, in the small surf, the pebbles grind and grate underfoot. I bend to them, they shine. A palmful of fine pebbles, polished like glass beads. Throw them into the water in a curve, a gull's wing of water drops. A fish jumps.

This place is a dump. We're not away from it all at all. We're not away from anything. "It" has been dumped here. Here is everything we put up with during the other fifty weeks of the year: chrome and vinyl, the smell of gas, the drone of the fridge, arborite and plastic. Styrofoam. Slough.

There's a black vinyl sofa and a metal-legged table topped with formica in a pattern of gold stars. It should be fifties' vintage but it's new. On the table there's a vase of bobbly glass. It contains a menu from the Pizzaria in the town thirty kilometres away. Would anyone really drive thirty kilometres for one of their number nineteens, summer sausage sizzler, or one of their twenty-sevens, deluxe double deli combo?

Too late. Someone has suggested it. Think of a number.

"I'll have a three."

"Food?" says Paddy. "Wouldn't let the stuff past my teeth," and takes another drink. Gail is looking for an outlet for her amp. We won't even have to listen to the wind.

The rocks are the place to be. Down there. Energy of millennia stored up. Massage the soles of your bare feet with it. Feel the vibes. A million messages of now, of then, trapped in the lichen, waiting for the satellite dishes of your cells.

Wait under the coral trunk of the arbutus. Listen while the wind shakes the clusters of hollow flowers, rattles them, breaks them in showers of papery beads. The water stops dancing and I lean out from the rock. The fish are there, turning under the surface, swimming round and round, waiting for the shudder of warm skin against scales, dreaming their martyr's dream of burning air. My hands close round cold, quick sides. In the air the fish bends once as if to swallow its own tail and then it straightens, is dead as it hits the rock. I lay it on a piece of cedar, carry it to the fire pit. I give thanks.

But we are not thinking of leaving. We are unpacking the ice-chests, packing the fridge.

"Did you bring salami, too? That makes three packages."

"Put some on the pizza."

Triple salami combo. There's too much food. And look at the booze. For two weeks? Cases of beer, mountains of chip bags. A monster bargain pack of crackers, the box as big as a suitcase.

"Want some dip? I could chop some onion in."

Oh, yes, do that. Keep busy. Whatever we do, let's keep busy and perhaps we won't notice the hairy old men at the door with bones in their noses.

The others are unpacking their bags, their books, cameras. Jen has brought her hair dryer, says we can all use it. After the beach. Paddy is on the couch, head back, arms extended along the back, eyes closed, smiling. Breathing deeply. The man who talks about the green hills back home, wild skies. We could be down there now. We could be picking up clam shells; I could be running my thumb in the grooves, turning them over to see the mussel and egg-yolk colours of the lining. Shining. Silk in the sun. We could be walking now on the wet sand with its slick of clouds. We could turn our faces to the wind, let the turning of the world suck the words from our mouths.

I unwrap the fish from the leaves charred now like bark. I pick off the falling flesh, burning my fingers and lips. It is sweet and oily.

The fire is small now, the eye of a star in the darkness, the eye of a fish in the deep. I feed it dry twigs and make it flare while I draw moss and feathery hemlock into the circle of light and make a bed. At the foot the fish bones. I lie down, breathe the dark.

Already we let our possessions possess the place, marking territory, marking time. The beach figures hardly at all.

"Is it far?"

Yes, it's far. It's two million years away in the quiet before we came.

"You wouldn't like it anyway, Mitch. Water, water everywhere and no Labatt's to drink."

"Did someone say beer?"

"You've got one."

"Are you counting?"

Talk, talk. The same as keeping busy. Don't let in the silence of the old men, the voices of the old women.

"Jude would have a walk to the beach. She's a fitness freak."

"Not tonight. There's a hockey game, remember?"

"And no TV, remember?"

Now what are they doing? Driving the van round to the front?

"Cannucks are ahead now. This is gonna be the kind of showdown we haven't seen in years. What do you say, Frank?" Tin voice of the tin man through the open tin doors of the van.

We sit on the porch, with the shower curtain tied back, and settle in for the game. I don't want to be here.

Down on the edge of the inlet the wind will be carrying memories, voices of the children we were flying like birds on it, voices rustling in darkness, in firelight, under the moon.

A woman walks towards me. The fish bones are in her hand. She squats beside me, wrapping her blanket tighter round and begins slowly to speak. She tells me stories of war, of death, of love. They are the stories of the rainforest, of the outback, of the hills of Wiltshire. I see slaves asleep with lords, like babies, wives, like warriors, letting blood. Deer I see, kneeling like virgins, bending under the knife, infants like lovers at the breast, fainting, infants born as animals die, in secret. I see old men shed tears. I see shadows like wings. The old woman fingers the fish bones as she speaks, she tells them like beads. And in her hands they turn to water and trickle away to make dark stains on the earth before they disappear.

It's early and very quiet. I'm cold. It must have rained in the night because the fish-print shower curtain dripped on my sleeping bag. But someone's been up already. There's a greasy pan resting precariously on the coffee mugs and glasses and last night's plates in the sink, and the kettle is warm. A small space is cleared between the wine bottles and the ashtrays on the counter and there's a bit of cold bacon left behind.

In the room with the couch, there's a stale smell. The drapes don't meet and a dust-laden sunbeam bores its way through to illuminate the beer stains and cigarette ash on the coffee table. I can hear snoring. No one picked up the playing cards that Paddy sprayed through the air during his conjuring trick. Before he fell over.

And we've only been here one day.

Oblivion. The old woman could give you oblivion. Tonight let her tell you stories that turn bones to water. She will tell you while you sleep, paint your faces and mine in blood and light the fire that will bubble us black. Forgive us all our forgetting.

A figure is coming through the trees, through the bars of morning light. Whistling. It is a thin sound, small and alone. But it is there nevertheless, a single consciousness unflinching against the giant presence of sea and tree.

Banging on the porch, sand out of shoes. A sneaker flying in. Then another.

"And they never found the body . . ." Paddy, sepulchral, from outside. Fool.

He leers in. Wild hair, salt-stung cheeks. Smiling. Necessary fool.

"Beach is great!" Drunken buffoon. Up and out without me, before me, and no rites necessary. Up and out and walking at the edge of time, the pouding of it in his ears, the fine spray of it wetting his eyes. His own private audience with the ocean.

"Thought it might be. Want some bacon?"

"I've had some."

"I know."

"Counting again."

"I'm always counting." That's my trouble. Counting and watching. Listening, but not hearing the thin, small sound of our living.

The bones are still there. Then there is no sacrament and fish itself is the only grace, the only mystery. Food for the body. And giving is love. Simple. Simple and beautiful. It is beautiful enough, this circle of life. I gather the bones and carry them down to the water's edge.

THE DEVIL AND THE DEEP

EVERY MORNING, PETER THOMAS WOULD GET UP AND LOOK OUT at the limpid beauty of the blue hills and the shining strait.

And every morning, the old man would be there on the sloop, clambering about like a gangly crab amid the shrouds and making ready to cast off from his mooring.

Peter Thomas would watch for a while, staring at the bent figure that was diminished and flattened by the distance and the light until it was little more than a shadow; then he would sigh at the remote grace of the scene, the near impossibility of it, drink a great breath of the startling air and go and shave.

And when he returned, every morning, from the bathroom, the old man would be gone, the water undisturbed and only a small skiff balancing on the surface of its flat light.

Peter Thomas lived an ordered life. He lived alone, was just and moral, fair to his fellow man and wrathful to his enemies. Of late, finding that it suited his time of life, he attended church with zeal; it made his Sundays more complete.

There were few things that he questioned. The old

man, however, bothered him. He would have liked to know where he went every day, what he did. Every day. And, he had begun to notice, there was something else: whether he himself rose early or late seemed to make no difference; whenever he went to the window and opened the shutters there the old man would be, making ready.

The coincidence became irksome; it was too obvious to go unnoticed, too marked to ignore, so that eventually he came to watch for it, randomly altering his routine by an hour, a few minutes, a morning, noting always the times and the tides but finding no pattern to the old man's time of sailing—other than a perfect correspondence with his own observation of it. If he kept to his bed and rose well past noon, then, as always, the old man would be there out in the strait, setting sail.

Peter Thomas went away for a few days.

When he returned, he walked with slow deliberation through the house to his room overlooking the narrows. He knew what he would see.

It was high summer and the tide was very low. He walked down to the beach. The sloop lay just off the uncovered rocks. The old man was bending over in it with his back to Thomas.

"So glad you could come," he called. "Stay there."

And before Thomas could reply, he had turned and was climbing into his skiff. With long, even strokes that seemed not to touch the water he pulled the small rowboat alongside the rock and held it steady.

"I do beg your pardon," he said, looking up. His eyes were an unpleasant weed-green but he was smiling gently. "I took you for someone else."

"Never mind," he added blithely. "Would you care to sail?"

"Well—" began Thomas.

"Good. Come along." And Thomas found himself climbing into the skiff.

He sat uneasily in the stern, holding the sides with both hands.

At the boat he was compelled to let the older man assist him. He climbed awkwardly on board. He stood uncertainly for a moment while the old man busied himself with lines and cleats and sent a sail wriggling aloft. At this Thomas sat down quickly and, before he knew what was happening, the sail had hung itself upon a wind that had sprung from nowhere, and they were underway.

And now something in the old man's manner—something not quite imperious but commanding nevertheless—made all of Thomas's questions seem out of place. He began to feel faintly seasick as the sloop picked up speed.

"I don't believe we've introduced ourselves," he said.

"But you know, of course, who I am, Mr. Thomas." The old man's voice was strong against the wind and he stared at Thomas without blinking.

Peter Thomas began to sense the full speed of the boat beneath him and his seasickness turned to vertigo; not only the water but time itself seemed to be slipping blackly under the hull, peeling away from them irretrievably. Thomas could not look at it. He could not look at the old man's dark and leathered face or the weed-green eyes. He turned his face to the sky. It was blackening with cloud.

It was hard to speak against the wind. His words were beaten back into his mouth until he was choking on them. But still he had to ask the question.

"What do you want?"

The wind boomed in the emptiness of the old man's silence and then quite suddenly fled away whining to the distant hills, leaving the sloop rocking in its wake.

The old man, one hand still on the tiller, squinted at Thomas. "I'm sorry?" he said and put the other hand up to his ear in an absurd gesture of frailty. He was an old, brittle man again, and Thomas's panic died down with the waves. He shook his head.

"It doesn't matter," he was saying, but the old man's fingers had closed like the pincers of a crab around his arm and he was being urged to look at something over the side.

Thomas looked. The calm water, inked by the cloud

overhead, was bottomless, black. Far down, hanging in deep space, was a whiteness.

Thomas thought it was shoal of fish drifting in the current but as some of them broke free and rose, tilting, towards the surface, he saw that they were faces. Hundreds upon thousands of them, pale and watching and twisting as they floated.

Thomas turned but already the old man was at work dragging a heavy net into place. He secured some lines and motioned to Thomas to help him heave the net over the side.

In no time at all the net was filled and they brought the catch to the surface. The air was alive with a gasping, a mouthing like a million bubbles and, as Thomas watched helplessly, the white faces dissolved into sheer phosphorescence and were blown away, sparkling dust motes on the rising wind.

He felt unaccountably angry.

"What earthly reason could you have," he demanded, "for what you've just done?"

The old man raised his eyebrows in polite surprise.

"My goodness! Isn't it obvious? I've saved them no end of misery. No end."

The logic of this reply eluded Peter Thomas.

"But there's nothing left. You've destroyed them."

"Come now. 'Destroyed' is a bit thick. One can't actually, metaphysically speaking, 'destroy' a soul; it is merely transferred from one state to another. These, I think, are fortunate. They have been incorporated in the universal stuff of life."

Thomas was not convinced. He remained angrily silent. They were picking up speed again, heading into the wind with a whine threading the rigging high above them. Thomas no longer recognized the coastline. Up ahead the strait narrowed and turned, so that they appeared to be sailing into an inlet where the clouds were piling over the hills. The old man seemed to feel compelled to justify himself.

"You see," he went on, "if I can put it this way, they're much better off where they belong, back at square one. What on earth do they want with this little, tiny, bite-down-or-it-will-hurt life when there's only eternity to follow. What goes on there, you know, is quite beyond anyone's control. Except His."

They were sailing so fast now that the sea seemed to rile and buck beneath them like a black horse trying to rid itself of a rider.

"Come now. You do follow, don't you?" said the old man. "Judgement Day and all that? Half of them make it, half of them don't. Personally I can't see the point."

Thomas said nothing but clung to the rail and tried to smother a rising sea-sickness.

Without warning the old man leaned forward and released the mainsheet and suddenly they were becalmed, as before, on the brow of a gently tossing sea.

As he heaved the net over again the old man looked at Thomas kindly.

"It's all for His benefit, you know. The whole thing. I saw that long ago. Oh, very long ago.

"Oh, he did some wonderful things: the stars, the hair on a doe's neck, the scent of crab apple. I could go on. But what's the use. He didn't make them to last. It's all rather cruel, I feel."

Thomas wiped the spray from his face and the tears that the wind had made, and watched the white shadows filling the net under the water.

"I know how you feel," he heard the old man saying. "All the suffering and the hurt. Someone has to be responsible. When I think . . . ah, but it's too painful. That's why I do them this kindness."

Again the net was hauled to the surface and again the air was filled with sighs as the white faces burst and were dispersed in clouds of shining colour.

When Thomas looked down, he found his hands, his arms, his chest covered with phosphorescence, and he was filled with disgust.

"You don't know," he said to the old man's back as he bent to untangle the net. "You don't know how I feel."

The old man looked up at him pleasantly, politely.

"Oh?" he said.

"Couldn't you at least give them a chance?" asked Thomas. "Life is full of suffering, yes, but there's happiness too, and they have a right to expect something more to follow."

"But exactly!" exclaimed the old man. "That's just what I've been saying. Take these things," and he shook out the residue from the net. "There was a time when they were perfectly comfortable in their oblivion. Then they had life foisted on them, inflicted on them, like fire on open flesh, and they *burn* with it. There's this longing and the need and pain and even love, and they remember it. All. And finally, when the whole show is over, what do they get? Eternity."

" 'Ah,' you say, 'that wouldn't be so bad.' But they don't all make it to the good part and those that do find it's really no great shakes after all. There's memory too, don't forget. Memory. An eternity of memories and no possibility of ever going back. Unbearable."

"No, they're much better off when I've finished with them."

Thomas let his hand trail in the dark water and watched the thin tails of phosphorescence stream from it like hair. Every breath he took seemed a prelude to a reply but, overcome with despondency, he said nothing.

For many hours they sailed, flying over the water, sometimes in darkness, sometimes in sun, but always with a wind that blew when it was summoned and dropped at the old man's command.

At last Thomas spoke again.

"It shouldn't have to be like this," he said.

"I know, I know," said the old man. "And I'd have arranged it otherwise if I'd been able."

Thomas looked at him sharply.

"But He's so much more powerful than I."

"What are you saying?" asked Thomas.

"I'm saying exactly what you think I'm saying. And you? Do you know where you stand, Mr. Thomas?"

There was a terrifying silence like the heat of the sun all around them.

"Just whose side would you say you were on, Mr. Thomas?"

But Peter Thomas could only stammer uncontrollably.

"Listen," said the old man, assuming his most reassuring, his most fatherly, tone. "The whole difficulty lies in your clinging to the notion of beneficent God. Suppose it were otherwise. Suppose for a moment that your Prime Mover is not all-good but all-evil. Would he advertise his pernicious nature? No. The kind of force we are up against is cunning beyond belief. So cunning he has you standing on your head and believing you see things right side up."

Thomas shook his head in disbelief.

"But that's diabolical," he said.

"Quite so," replied the old man.

Thomas looked wildly about him as if for help. He turned again to the head of the inlet to where the clouds were heaped in a fearful mass, the molten light of the sun pouring through them onto the flat sea like water through the cracks in a dam. Night closing or the cataracts of dawn, Thomas had no way of knowing.

BLIND SPOT

BRINK INSIDE HIS BODY QUELLED A RISING PANIC, KNEW EVEN with his eyes shut, that he was not in his own room, guessed at once that it had been another stroke. He felt the leaking of cold fear between the joints of his elbows, his ankles, a watery trickling in his knuckles. Breathe, breathe.

And he did, he could.

He was lying on his back. His mouth was dry. He swallowed. Gingerly he touched one foot with the other. His first stroke had left one side of his foot numb; he had recovered the feeling in a matter of weeks, bragged about the power of his mind. But he was not numb. Then what? His body moved, stretched, turned. He made it sit up and reach for the buzzer, make it speak—'Nurse?'—and it was in perfect accord with his thought and right on cue. But God he needed water.

Nothing worse to suffer than the sound of a torrent between his ears and a landslide behind his eyes when he moved suddenly. He had known hangovers worse.

Brink then besotted with his luck, drunk on it. Brink who loved irony reaping a fitting reward for years of staunch resistance to good advice, decades of steadfast loyalty to a pack a day and the scorching pleasure of rye. Brink vindicated.

The doctor in retaliation would not let him get up, his spectacular recovery clearly regarded as precocious, presumptuous even. And Brink, complying with the bedpan, was more than pleased to hear the admonishing edge to the nurse's voice, the sharp edge they used on healthy patients.

But then Shelagh. Quick as ever to interfere with his pleasure. Apt that his ex-wife should derail his illusions. As always.

One of the nurses (there seemed to be so many . . .) one of them anyway came to tell him that a Shelagh Heath had called at the desk and was coming in. Her name summoned the whole familiar mix of excitement and dismay. Well he was a sick man and she had better remember it.

He looked up when he heard the door open with a soft puff of air. But there was only a strange woman looking in so he smiled briefly and glanced down again at his tea, assuming that she was looking for another patient.

"George!" At the sound of his ex-wife's voice he looked up again but there, again, was only the strange woman and she was coming towards his bed.

"George. I've only just heard." She held out her hand to him and she spoke with Shelagh's voice. "This is a bad habit you're acquiring."

He stared and stared at the thin red lips and the small teeth, scanning them as if with trying he would be able to see the familiar voice issuing from the strange opening. He began to feel sick. The walls were in motion. He heaved himself out of bed, lurched to the bathroom and vomited hard.

One of the nurses arrived. She made him sit on the floor with his head between his knees. When he came out of the bathroom, Shelagh had gone.

Afterwards, in the quiet of the darkened hospital room, Brink began to piece things together. He knew exactly where he was. The Peninsula hospital. How many staff would serve this floor? Not more than two, three at the most. It was the same faces he had been seeing over and over. Or not seeing. To put it accurately, it was *different* faces. He had been seeing different faces on the same people. He had recognized, could recognize, no one.

The obvious question occurred to him. His hands went up to his face but he was afraid to touch.

Carefully, trying not to trigger a landslide, Brink made his way again to the bathroom. When he reached the sink, he held on to the basin, looked up slowly, slowly, to the mirror and saw, as he knew he would, a stranger's face tilting slowly, slowly, to meet his own. The same minute lesion, the same crack in the microchip that had sent him reeling and confused down to the dock three days previously, had erased quite cleanly his ability to recognize any human face at all.

The boat man appeared to be not the usual man. Of this Brink was almost sure, the voice a stranger's, not seeming to know him. It was a relief. He settled back, let his face stare slackly into the uncertain light. The launch drilled the gull-coloured mists.

A relief to be at last a stranger in his turn. A chance now to get back without seeing anyone. Without anyone seeing him. He had told no one he was checking himself and his face out of the hospital. Who to tell?

The island detached itself from the mist. No one on the dock. Thank God, thank God. For nothing. He thanked the boat man, paid him and climbed out, and the launch turned, heading back to the mainland, left a slap of glassy water against the dock, a smell of gas hanging in the air.

Brink set out for his cottage. It was on the unforgiving north side of the island where the rock abutted a scoop of stony beach. Hard to say whether his work had taken on the character of his surroundings or whether he was like the dog-owner who comes to resemble the dog. In any event, Brink lived alone. His cottage was rough and unfinished and filled randomly with furniture he had either made or scavenged. There had been women, two or three, and Shelagh. They had left behind them various books, bits of pottery forsaken in the hasty retreat from hostile country.

The earth all heavy from the spring rain clung to his boots but when he reached his door he went straight in. Purposeful. About to surprise and orgy in progress, brigands counting loot. Everything was exactly as he had left it three days before, except that the radio was bubbling weakly from the kitchen table and the coffee had dried to a dark brown stain in the bottom of the pot. Signs of life almost extinguished. He walked by them both, went straight to the mirror that hung in the bathroom, and took it down.

There was another mirror, a large one in his room. His hands were shaking as if he had had a night of drinking. He ransacked the kitchen drawer for tape, found some, found a newspaper and managed somehow to cover over the glass, leaning his head against the paper to hold it in place while his fingers picked at the tape. Hands shaking now as if his wrists had been cut. When it was done he poured himself a large brandy, scrawled an entry in his notebook: *"Who's been asking the questions?"* and went to bed.

The sheets were damp and cold. Brink kept his clothes on, covered himself with an extra blanket from the couch. Got up again for the brandy bottle. He had never shivered so much but still it was exhausting and in the end wore him down.

To let go of the mind, a feat more terrifying than free fall. In the moment before sleep, and just as he had dreaded, a face appeared behind his closed eyes, and hung there (it might have been a lover's—or his own—he felt such sudden longing) but when sleep came it was as he had hoped it would be: empty and blank as amnesia.

And his sleeping face upon the pillow, just as harmless: intact, unmarked; properly proportioned; squarish under cropped grey hair, decently weathered, the right amount of living inscribed in lines not too ugly; something cynical about the jaw perhaps, about the eyes, too, something soft and puffy, dissolute, but all in all a good face—had he only been able to recognize it. For he had tried. Just before he left the hospital he had stared and stared at the mirror above the basin. But he could not persuade his brain.

Despite his amnesiac sleep, Brink woke early to a complete and sharp consciousness of his new condition. He had a headache to rival the most poisonous hangover and, what was more disturbing by far, he had an acute awareness of the flesh and skin that covered the front of his skull. He was looking at the world through the eyeholes of a mask that twitched and puckered independently. He let his eyes do their looking through the holes.

In this room he both slept and worked. His bed took up one side of the room. In front of the window was a trestle table he had made himself from pine boards, wide enough to accommodate acres of papers and sturdy enough to withstand his thunderous assaults on the typewriter. Drawn up to it was a shabby dining chair which Brink favoured for its height and its padded back and seat. It was covered in red upholstery, faded and worn. Where he had spent—wasted?—half a lifetime probing the question of identity.

Identity was a myth: he knew that. He had asserted it time and again. It was apparent in everything he wrote. Individuality was simply the projection of a particular neurochemical composition. His favourite analogy for the human condition was the ant heap; human relations were mere formication. Desire was nothing more than a rush of epinephrine, love merely a surfeit of oxytocin. There was no capacity in the ant for soul, no room in the ant heap for God.

Brink had once declared, with uncharacteristic tolerance, that God might exist or not, just as God chose. The question was of no consequence. It was blind men debating the light from a distant star.

His books, needless to say, were not hot items in the stores. There was one which enjoyed a brief run but its title, 'Formication,' and the publisher's decision to place a picture of naked men and women under it was almost certainly the only factor in its success. The rest of his work remained, unappetizing and aloof, on the shelves, like bottles of cod liver oil at the back of the medicine cabinet —like Brink in his spartan cottage.

Across from the bed was the only other piece of furniture, a triple-doored armoire so vast it took up all of one wall. An exile from some straitened family home, it was entirely out of place in Brink's room. He had, besides, only one jacket to hang. The wardrobe did, however, house a great number of manuscript files, heaped on the shelves behind each of the side doors and crammed into the drawers below.

From his bed by the window, Brink let his eyes stare unmoving at the Saturday paper taped across the middle of the thing, for a large, bevelled glass was set there in the centre door.

Three steps across the room and he could remove the paper.

He got up without looking at the paper again. He washed and dressed and made a pot of coffee. Then he sat in the kitchen warming his hands round the cup, not sure whether he could yet sit at his desk with the great mirror behind him.

As an answer to Brink's endless probing into the question of identity, this sudden and complete removal of perhaps its only tangible projection was a spitefully accommodating trick of fate. He had not before thought of irony as spiteful.

He had worked only for clarity, had hoped only to cast light. All his life he had tried to explain away the inexplicable, to demystify mystery. And now his nerve failed him.

It was as if a ghost, tired of having its existence called into question, had walked out of the house forever, leaving him to die of loneliness. His voice echoed through aeons of emptiness: "This is your captain speaking/This is your captain speak/This is your captain . . ."

The crack in the microchip had left him with more than a cerebral blind spot. It had stalled his whole programme.

He was not sure how long he had been sitting at the kitchen table. The last of his coffee was cold. He could see the flat image of a face darkly reflected on its surface. He was not afraid of the strange features that waited in the mirror. It was not that. It was something that would *not* be there.

He knew he could come to terms with his condition. Already he had thought it through, anticipating the feeling of vulnerability that would come from being always and everywhere surrounded by strangers, realizing that they might smile like friends but would remain unrecognizable however many times they appeared—like the faces of surgeons hovering over the not quite anaesthetized patient. But, he was a rational man, the prospect was not insupportable. He could learn in time to impose some meaning on the jumbled and indeterminate features of a face. He could, at the very least, teach his brain to bypass its dependence there and look for other signs, other announcements of identity, if only...

If only. ... He tried to avoid the unproductive words. He lit a cigarette. He disliked the touch of his lips on his hands and so he put the cigarette in the ashtray and watched the smoke twist and vanish through a shaft of sunlight.

If only there had been something there. But he had looked in the eyes. There had been nothing.

Just as he had always said.

The sun was shining brightly into the room. Its reflection from the water outside made ripples like heatwaves on the ceiling. The newspaper that covered the mirror smelled hot and had already yellowed. Brink stared for a long time at the ordered blocks of words. His hand reached out to the tape and began to peel it, sticky and creaking from the wood. His hands lifted the newspaper away and, for a second, in the brilliance, Brink thought he saw a face but there was nothing, only the blinding splash where the sun had lasered in from the sea and split itself against the glass.

BLOODY DOG

IT WAS NOT A PARTICULARLY LARGE DOG, NO LARGER THAN A Dobermann. But it was black and its eye—for it did had only one—was yellow. Its ears—two—were almost as sharply pointed as its teeth, which were extraordinarily white. And long. There was too a certain air about it, attributable no doubt to its single watchful eye, a look of such highly-strung preparedness that one could not help noticing these things. Like the teeth. The way they seemed to start of their own accord from the jagged black lips.

Merely to look at this dog could provoke the most mild mannered observer to vicious execrations and sometimes even to violence. A plumber—"Your Home's Best Friend," as the side of his van proclaimed—took one look at the unfortunate animal as it stood with its hackles prickling, decided that the chicken-wire fence was not sufficiently robust, and hurled a solid cast drain trap over it before he ran. The drain trap broke the kitchen window.

She had found the dog in the pound. The officer there had raised an eyebrow when she said she wanted to have a look at it. "Beauty's in the eye . . ." he said sullenly. He had his arm in a sling but that might have been a coincidence. He brought the dog out on a long chain. Its legs were shaking so much that it sat down—one of the few times in its life it was seen to do so. It held the powerful canines over its lower lip the way humans do with their front teeth when they deal with slugs or spiders or old spaghetti.

"Ah," she said with compassion. "What is it?"

"Mongrel," said the officer with some energy.

"Ah!" she said again and then, "Ah!"

"Lucky dog!" she thought she heard the officer mutter as they pushed it front first, resisting, into the car—but she might have been mistaken.

Her choice, when the dog finally emerged from under the garden shed where it spent its early days, amazed, not to say startled, her friends. Without exception they found their introduction to the beast distressing. By this time it had gained a considerable degree of confidence.

Most traumatic of all was meeting it on its home turf. The front door of the house was at the top of a flight of steps overlooked by a window. At the first sound of a shoe on the bottom step the dog would claw its way across the slippery floor, knock a few plants off the window sill and stand on its hind legs. With forelegs stiff on the edge of the sill and the white flea collar showing beneath its yabbering jaw, it looked like nothing less than a werewolf masquerading as the local vicar.

Visitors to the house, those who knew, kept their head down as they mounted the steps; those taken by surprise backed down again and called instead from somewhere near the scarlet runners. It was only for the stout-hearted to wait at the front door where the scrabbling and the slavering from the other side increased in intensity with every new wave of adrenaline that pulsed in through the mail slot.

"Oh, come in," she'd say. "Don't stand there shivering."

Some stopped coming. One moved to Prince George. Which was quite far away. But Doggy's mistress—she'd named it Doggy after rejecting several suggestions from friends—hardly noticed, so full had her life become.

Although when they went for walks Doggy was liable to stop other amblers in their tracks—"What *is* that?" or, sometimes, "What is *that?*"—he really was a most rewarding pet. He jumped like a bird for sticks, bicycling in thin air to gain height, and he rocketed like a ground-launched missile after balls; he could whimper with delight and groan with disappointment and altogether melt with longing for his Beefie Bitz. But most important he listened with undiscriminating attention to every word his mistress said. Practically.

He was the perfect distraction from the shrinking circle of friends he had decimated, and that his mistress should soon find him indispensable was thoroughly natural; the two of them became inseparable.

It was just unfortunate people said. But then again they had seen it coming. They had seen it coming from so far away they had begun to take precautions long before it arrived.

Thanks to PW Travis.

Policewoman Travis was the name she gave her new neighbour, a big, strapping woman with dogs of her own. And a whistle. The dogs were nice happy creatures that bounced around as if they were after the lead in a Bonio commercial. The whistle was a 'Thunderer'. Whenever PW Travis was out with her dogs the air would be punctured with shrill blasts of the Thunderer as it called her dogs to order: one blast for 'Come', two for 'Sit', five for 'Stop it at once'. There they would be, halfway to a good sniff with a springer spaniel when—"Preep!"—they would be arrested, yes arrested is the word, in mid-stride like figures in an instant replay. It would have been no surprise at all to see them running backwards.

The neighbourhood began to shape up when PW arrived. First she erected a Berlin wall between her property and Doggy's. She put broken glass on top. Next she petitioned Doggy's mistress to fortify the boundaries of Doggy's territory—for the protection of others. She had forty-two signatures on her petition.

Doggy's mistress looked at Doggy in a new light. Now she noticed little things that had escaped her: the way the milkman mopped his brow when he called with the bill, the way young mothers snatched their charges from the sidewalk when Doggy approached.

She decided Doggy needed social rehabilitation and began to drive him to the park. But it was no good; it was as if she had a siren on the roof of her car wailing a two minute warning as she drove in. Boxers would be bundled into station wagons, terriers into tweed bosoms, and the place would become a desert before Doggy had lifted a leg. At last a little handwritten message on blue note paper was left on her windshield: *With all due respect, there are those among us who would very much appreciate it if you would kindly keep your dog on a leash. Thank you. P.S. Or walk elsewhere.*

Doggy's mistress didn't mind. For a while she kept Doggy on a leash but he took to lying down when he saw another dog approaching. He would drop at once to his belly flattening himself into the grass and advancing with a strange quick shifting movement. And it didn't seem to help his bewilderment one bit when dogs, and even people, skirted their path in a wide circle, or sometimes turned and went back the way they had come.

There were those, PW Travis among the first, who took to carrying staves, sauntering in a vain attempt at nonchalance, as if they carried nothing more hefty than walking canes.

Doggy's mistress at last began to mind. If they didn't want to socialize, they didn't. She took Doggy instead to the airport. At least you couldn't intimidate a 707.

In the wide open spaces beyond the runway Doggy would barrel along for miles, his feet rototilling the short wiry turf, larks and grouse spurting in all directions like shrapnel. He took to hunting rabbits. She took to cooking them. They ate together.

It was just unfortunate, they said afterwards, that the corgi happened to be at the right place at the wrong time. Or was it the other way round?

It was one of those high, windblown days when the ground flattens its ears under the roar of the sky. Bored with rocketing around to no avail, Doggy had been running splay-legged, nose down for almost half an hour when the corgi broke cover. To Doggy, the sight of its white scut bouncing like a live tennis ball in the distance was like a match to blue touch-paper. He shot away, his legs forming a single, spinning wheel on which he hurtled to—one had to suppose—the little dog's doom.

The people in the little red Honda, that she saw for the first time, clawed their way out and stood clutching each other in a dumb show of horror.

The two animals disappeared into a dip beyond a low ridge. Doggy's mistress closed her eyes. The Honda people opened their mouths. No sound came out.

In no more than a moment Doggy trotted back over the ridge, his tail pluming in the air in explicit elation and his jaw working over something gristly in his mouth.

The man ducked inside the car and reappeared wielding a staff as thick as his wrist.

Doggy's mistress felt her knees go weak. Doggy's knees however, reacted like plucked catgut and once more he was off, flying over the grass with his tail tucked in for safety and the man's abuse pelting after him like a hail of rotten tomatoes.

"Killer! Bloody, vicious, bloody, no-good killer! Bloody dog!"

He turned and Doggy's mistress braced herself for his attentions but they were brief. "You better find it before I do," he said, "that's all. Come on, Winnie." He grabbed his wife's elbow and Winnie, looking white, hopped obligingly beside him as he set out across the field.

Doggy's mistress decided that it would not be altogether to her dog's disadvantage to have a home-base and she declined to go on the search, saying she would remain behind at the roadside in case he was circling back.

It wasn't long before the couple reappeared over the ridge. Winnie, looking whiter than ever, was clearly a handicap when it came to stalking prey.

"Not the last you'll hear of it by a long chalk," said the man. "I'm coming back. With some help."

Doggy's mistress said nothing. She thought she knew where Doggy might be.

When the man had gone, she drove her car round to an abandoned shed that stood a little way off to the side beyond the low ridge. As she made her way over to the hut she was surprised that the man hadn't heard the whimpering. Or perhaps he had.

Walking round to the back, she got down on her hands and knees and looked under. The whimpering changed key and one yellow eye peered at her out of the gloom. The dog, grey with thick cobwebs from the bottom of the hut, looked like a moth-eaten wolf.

His ears, no longer pricked, were crumpled with fear and he seemed to hold his jaw all askew.

"Doggy, Doggy, Doggy," she called brightly. But it was no use; whether she called brightly, or firmly, or even desperately Doggy didn't come.

The light was going fast and it was getting very cool. She shivered. There was nothing else for it but to crawl under and push him out.

She was halfway under when she heard the truck. The engine stopped. She knew it had stopped by her car. She scrambled in beside Doggy and through a crack in the skirting she looked out over the flat ground. There were three of them getting out, silhouetted against the fading light, and there was no mistaking the way they carried their sticks.

The dog winced as she put her hand on his nose. "Shut up!" she hissed.

They waited. For the first time she noticed that there were pieces of fur on the ground. It was hard to see the colour and rabbit might look a lot like corgi in the dust, but it *was* pale fur. And thick. And it was all in small pieces.

Well, whatever he'd done, she wouldn't let them take him without a fight.

But perhaps she wouldn't be the only one to fight. Perhaps Doggy was going to rally. Perhaps he was going to go out in a spectacular vindication of all things ugly and maligned, thunder growling in his dark throat, lightning striking from his yellow eye, a conflagration of all the maledictions heaped upon him, a maelstrom of black fur, and both canines blazing.

THE TURN OF THE YEAR

WINTER

At the far northern tip of the island, where small farms ploughed right up to the hemlock woods, lived Hannah and her young son, Joseph.

INTERIOR HANNAH'S HOUSE FRONT ENTRANCE LATE DAY
HANNAH is dressing JOSEPH and herself for the cold, pulling on hat, boots etc.. HANNAH concentrates on the clothes, trying not to look too much at the boy. On the floor beside them, there is a suitcase round which a large Irish wolfhound worries excitedly. The sound of the dog's claws on the wooden floor is very distinct.

Hannah and her son were inseparable. He was all she had, she told herself fiercely and without sentiment. To her husband Ted, she put the matter more succinctly. "If you take him away, you'll kill me," were the words she chose to use.

But one day her husband did take the child away, albeit with the sanction of the courts, and on that day Hannah did, in a manner of speaking, cease to be.

EXTERIOR HANNAH'S DRIVE DUSK SLEETY RAIN
From behind the closed window of the car JOSEPH is calling repeatedly:
—'Bye, Malachi! 'Bye, Malachi! 'Bye Malachi!
HANNAH, getting in, is muttering under her breath:
—Damn dog!

It was the last day of the year when she gave up her son, handing him over in the airport lounge, the goods delivered, and she drove home in a falling rain, the sky streaming, her eyes streaming, the cars thinning, getting fewer and fewer the farther she drove, until she was alone, heading out alone, for the north end of the island.

At six o'clock, the time the plane was due to take off, she switched on the radio, as if, should there be a crash, the news of it would somehow be relayed instantly and she would hear of it. But the radio only crackled and fizzed like a damp firework.

"Damn," said Hannah. "Damn radio. Damn rain. Damn dog. Damn airport. Damn husband." And then, as an afterthought: "Ex-husband."

She drove on. The road ahead was as black as the sky but Hannah thought only of the boy, saw him in sunshine, saw him running, light as a bird, laughing. She did not usually pray but tonight she addressed the whole wet night sky:

"Make him be safe. Make him be safe. Oh, God, if you're there, make him be safe."

INTERIOR HANNAH'S HOUSE EVENING
HANNAH is sitting with her feet drawn up on the edge of a chair, rocking. The dog, Malachi, lies with its chin pressed flat on the floor and watches her.

"Malachi!" Hannah made the dog jump with the sudden shrillness of her voice. "Malachi, I can't stand it! I'm going out—yes, O-U-T, walkies—and I'm going to be out there when that plane touches down two thousand miles away. I'm going to be *with* him."

EXTERIOR COUNTRY LANE NIGHT SLEETY RAIN
HANNAH is walking with the dog, reluctant now, at her heels. She is striding out, unconscious of the cold rain or of the depth of darkness on either side of the straggly hedgerows.

At exactly nine thirty-five she stopped. The sleet was no longer falling. The plane would have touched down.
Now.
Purposeful and calm, Hannah took a deep breath, turned round and started home. The rain had stopped; there was no sound but that of her own footsteps and the dog's. After the rustle of the sleet, the quiet of the December night was vast. It felt as if the sky had disappeared and the eye of God was watching from the emptiness beyond. It felt lonely beyond belief.
"Soon home, Malachi," said Hannah. But when she looked Malachi was not there. She whistled. There was no sound anywhere.
Cursing the dog under her breath, Hannah walked on. But there again was the sound of his paws on the gravel, as distinct as if he were by her side.
She stopped and whistled again, louder this time. The silence all around was so deep that she could, she thought, even hear his breathing. She walked on quickly, annoyed.
At the drive, she could still hear him, but the sound of his feet, his breathing, seemed to be growing more distant. The sounds were receding.
Hannah whistled now as loudly as she could. When she stopped, the only sound she heard, in all the world it seemed, was her own whistle echoing minutely inside her head.

INTERIOR HANNAH'S HOUSE KITCHEN MORNING
HANNAH is making breakfast. She is whistling softly, as if self-consciously. When the toast is ready she sits down and breaks it into a heap of tiny pieces.

It snowed in the night. When Hannah woke up, the walls and ceiling of her room were shining with reflected light. She stood at the window and looked out at the dazzling obliteration. There was nothing but mounding whiteness, blank, absolute.

Hannah went straight downstairs and opened the back door. The snow was unmarked by any tracks. Its light filled all the sky.

"No good whistling now, Malachi," she said softly, "is it?"

She had her breakfast of a mug of strong black coffee and took the toast out to the birds.

The rest of the day cannot be said to have passed as days do pass; it existed in a state of suspension, embalmed in snow.

To Hannah this seemed wholly appropriate, especially with Malachi gone. He'd taken himself off before like this. After some bitch in heat, she told herself. She did not like to think of him crunching rabbits and squirrels under the pine trees. She spent her time chopping wood and listening to mournful arias on the stereo. There was still no radio. When towards evening the loneliness of the previous night edged back and Hannah tried to call an old friend, she found the line was out of order and she was glad. "Good," she said and she stacked the stove full of wood and went to bed.

The dog did not return and Hannah began to feel uneasy in her isolation. With the snow already melted by a warm Pacific wind, the remains lying in patches under the hedges like shadows on a negative, Hannah drove up to the general store by the highway, watching out for Malachi on the way. The store was closed. That it should close for a few days after the New Year did not surprise Hannah. She still, nevertheless, needed milk.

"To the farm, James. To the farm." She turned abruptly to the empty seat beside her. "Not much of a wag, are you, James?" she said.

EXTERIOR A NEIGHBOUR'S FARM DAY
Lights are on in the farmhouse. There is a truck in the driveway; Hannah's car is parked by the truck. HANNAH is at the house. She knocks on a window and calls:
—Anybody home? Marg? Time to get up. Good party?
There is no answer and HANNAH walks over towards the barn.

It was disconcerting to find no animals. Hannah decided that the Bryces were away, their animals boarded at a friend's farm perhaps. It did not seem a very satisfactory explanation but it might—or it might not—account for the lights' being left on in a house that was all locked up. Hannah assumed it *was* all locked up. She was reluctant to try the door. It would not help, after all.

She got back in the car and began to reverse down the long drive.

"All right, James. We are not amused. A farm, James. Take me to a farm. One with geese and ducks . . . quack . . . and a fat pig . . . oink, oink . . . and above all . . . a great . . . big . . . mother of a cow so I can put some . . . *milk* in my coffee!"

And while she was at it, she thought, she could use the phone. She would call the police and see if any strays had been run over, picked up, sighted.

But the next farm was as quiet as the first. There were lights here too, a porch light and one at a side door. Hannah thought she heard the rusty squawk of a chicken but it was only a branch creaking as the wind squeezed it against the roof of a shed.

There were no animals. This time Hannah did not need to go and look.

Instead, she drove straight home and, once inside the house, went to the phone. It was still out of order. She could not stop the dial tone, no matter which numbers she tried to call.

"Who needs people?" she said and put the phone down shakily.

The next day Hannah made a list:
>   1. Find someone
>   2. Find Malachi
>   3. Find a phone
>   4. Find some milk

Pausing for a moment she wrote carefully:
>   5. I think you can cope, don't you?
>   6. Yes

She spent the rest of the morning visiting her neighbours, systematically. By lunch time she gave up.

Sitting in her kitchen again, warming her hands on a mug of black coffee and staring at the list, she had an urge to change number six from 'yes' to 'no'. Instead, she forced herself to be rational. It was a local evacuation. She told herself it had to be.

In the afternoon she drove out further, listening to the crackle of the radio, watching for cars that were not stationary, not empty. She found a service station, it too with its lights on, and filled her car with gas. There was no one to pay. She thought of leaving twenty dollars on the cash desk but she changed her mind and drove on. Once she thought she saw a bird fly up from beside the road, but it was only a dark scrap of paper, blown by the wind.

Again she returned home early in the precipitate dark, and this time she locked all the doors and double checked them.

EXTERIOR CORNER STORE WINTER MORNING
The end of a two-by-four smashes through the glass, setting the alarm ringing. HANNAH knocks out the rest of the glass to reach inside for the lock.

"And two litres of milk please. Cream? Why not?" Hannah had almost filled her box from the store's fridge. "I do think it adds a little oomph to a dreary can of peaches, don't you? I knew you'd agree. Eggs, thank you. Cheese, thank you. Thank you very much."

She pushed the full box along the floor, singing:
"Thank you very much for the food we're eating.
Thank you very much,
Thank you very, very, very, much."
At the door she lifted the box to carry it over the broken glass and out to the car.

EXTERIOR CORNER STORE BRIGHT WINTER SUN
The trunk is already full with three boxes of canned and dry goods. Hannah drives home without closing the trunk. The alarm in the store is still ringing.

SUMMER

EXTERIOR HANNAH'S GARDEN SUMMER DAY
HANNAH is seated at a table out of doors. She is dressed as for a summer luncheon. There are flowers on the table, and wine. Music is coming from the open windows of the house. HANNAH, very animated, is talking as she eats.

"Oh, it was dreadful, just *dreadful.* I couldn't believe it. Oh, yes. I drove all round the island. All round. Not a soul. Not . . . a . . . soul." She poured more wine. "You've no idea. Well, one just goes to pieces, absolutely to pieces. More salmon? Yes it is nice, isn't it? I was quite lucky to get hold of it."

She picked up the can of salmon and scraped the last flakes onto her plate. "What was I saying? Oh, yes. Well to begin with I just lay around in bed. You know how it is. I lived like a slut, really. Let everything go. Almost everything."

FLASHBACK TO:
INTERIOR HANNAH'S KITCHEN WINTER MORNING
HANNAH extremely disheveled in housecoat. Boxes, cartons of food all over the floor, dishes in the sink. Books, papers, dirty cups on every available surface. HANNAH removes a plate of food from a small oasis of order on the table. She scrapes it into a full garbage bag and puts a fresh plate in its place. She does the same with a

mug of milk, tips it away, replaces it. She repeats the procedure with the dog's food. Finally she slips her bare feet into boots and goes out to the garden with some bread. A midden of crusts has formed under the feeder.

"One thing, though," she leaned forward intently. "Do you know I never let go of the time. Not once. Oh, yes, incredibly difficult. Well, it's like being in solitary, tremendously difficult to keep track. But do you know what I did?"

She leaned further forward, secretive now and drunk. "I wrote his name—no, not Ted's—Joseph's. I wrote his name every day. Once every day. On the wall." Her gestures were grand. "When I came to my senses I had seventy nine 'Joseph's' to clean off. Can you imagine? In lipstick."

She took another drink of wine and looked up suddenly, in surprise, "Now? Well I use a calendar now just like anyone else. Oh, I know," she said, opening another can. "It's amazing what you can do when you put your mind to it. But I'm lucky. I have electricity, you see, and my wood stove. And my music. Do you like this? Gluck's *Chaconne*. Nice isn't it? I treated myself. It is my birthday after all. I went into town—I don't often get there these days—"

FLASHBACK TO:
EXTERIOR TOWN SUMMER DAY
HANNAH'S car is in the middle of the deserted street, the door of the car open. There is glass on the sidewalk; alarms are ringing. HANNAH is beside the car. She is turning round and round, screaming at the blank windows of the buildings.

"—and I picked up a few records.

"And I've planted a kitchen garden. And did I tell you I'm teaching myself navigation? From the library, of course. Well, I just let myself in. What else could I do. I stamp them out at least. Don't always get them back on time, though. Never did. Yes, the garden's doing very well, very well indeed. I'll let you have some raspberries this year; they're just full of bloom. Well I know there are no bees," she poured the last of the wine, "but they'll find a way. We manage without them, after all . . ."

INTERIOR BEDROOM NIGHT
HANNAH *is undressed. She is standing in front of a long mirror, her palms, her breasts, her forehead pressed to the glass. Her eyes are closed.*

WINTER

There had been times, of course, when Hannah had considered getting off the island. But during that first winter, when the seas were high, Hannah had been able to think of other, less uncomfortable ways to commit suicide, if it should come to that.

And the warmer calmer seas of summer had not made any difference; even when she had her boat equipped and ready to go, Hannah's feet stayed firmly planted on the island. If she ever did get away, she knew what she would find. Or, to be more accurate, not find. Clearly this was no bomb, nor evacuation, nor even epidemic.

Exactly what it was she was not sure. It had occurred to her that it was all her own doing, that she might indeed be in control. But still there was a small voice that came from a great distance and suggested that she might be in control, yes—for the time being—but she was nevertheless being watched, most closely.

Her rational mind told her bluntly that she was mad.

And yet she never gave in. It was not a question of courage; it was just that it would be like walking out of a movie—and Hannah always stayed until the end. How long it would take to reach the end of this one she did not know—but she was determined to see it through.

And so, from day to day, through all the surprising spring, throughout the green and leafy summer and on into the bitter, barren autumn, Hannah had continued to survive. Sometimes she would drive back to the deserted town, setting alarms ringing as she took what she wanted from the stores, music mainly, choral works that she played at full volume, sending the choirs like angel voices over the empty fields.

As the year wore on the feeling began to come to her, more and more often, of a day charged with a sense of imminence; Hannah would get up and set her house in an expectant kind of order, clearing the debris of her living from the rooms, resurrecting old rituals and settings that would pronounce reality.

But these days at their close were as barren as the plants outside.

Then, as the days grew colder, Hannah spent her time collecting wood to fill the stove; and she would sit there beside it, every day the same, listening to it, feeling its warmth, waiting, remembering.

EXTERIOR AIRPORT WINTER DUSK
The only sound is the wind. HANNAH is beside her car, shivering. She is staring through the fence at the empty terminal, the great planes abandoned on the tarmac like bugs frozen in the icy wind.

In time came the day she waited for, the last of the year.

She got up early. When dawn came it was a thinning of the dark, no more, and the day was drab and chill. Hannah walked for a while but the silence was too large and she returned to the house to sit in front of the stove again and listen to its soft roar. She stared at the heavy sky and she waited.

At about four o'clock the sun found a breach in the cloud and leaked its pink all over the west. Hannah decided that waiting was not enough. She could not last another year, would not live another day alone.

She put her head in her hands and closed her eyes. She had to make it work, would make it work. They were all there waiting in the falling dark, strangers, friends, lovers she had known, did not yet know, her son. . . .

She didn't know which to imagine first. She didn't know whether she should start with God. She didn't know if all she could imagine was herself imagining.

While her eyes were still closed, the first flakes of white drifted down on the dark.

Hannah started, so intently had she been listening for the sound of falling snow.

NOT AT THIS ADDRESS

ELIZABETH, INCONGRUOUS AGAINST THE BACKGROUND OF rusting hawthorn and darkening brambles, was suddenly and silently there in the gravel drive, the way a deer appears from nowhere. Elizabeth, however, was far from sylvan and it was not only her polyester raincoat with its swatch of blue and white at the neck, not only her shiny shoes; a deer, even a deer taken by surprise, would have had more confidence in its purpose. Here, on this country road edging a tall stand of fir, Elizabeth seemed uncomfortably aware of her own presence; she might almost have stepped off a bus at the wrong stop—except that there were no buses.

The young couple out walking after a pleasantly long Sunday lunch were momentarily startled by Elizabeth standing so oddly out of place in Miss Ridgley's drive.

"Mrs. Turnsbull's house?" asked Elizabeth, and her voice was strong and determined and altogether out of keeping with her hesitant manner as well as with her age, which was considerable.

Now, the couple who were out walking, that afternoon, aptly rustic in hiking boots and lumpy, mud-coloured sweaters, were clearly locals and they followed the lead of their older neighbours in maintaining if not a coldness then at least a damp chill towards outsiders. Elizabeth, wearing the raincoat unbuttoned as if she had no intention of staying out in the October air, and clutching a large vinyl handbag as if she had only a second ago expected to place it at the side of an armchair and take up a cup of tea, Elizabeth was plainly an outsider. In any event, neither of the couple enjoyed her tone of voice, peremptory, only a shade removed from demanding.

"Yes, down there on the right," said the young woman and twitched a sharp little smile onto her face.

"Where—exactly?" said Elizabeth, again in that short, haughty tone and despite the fact that she was staring in precisely the right direction. She was coming out towards them, walking with a limp, so that raincoat, handbag, blue and white flounce all flopped in time to her stiff, halting gait.

"On the right, Ma'am. Just down there," said the young man, turning away from her with conspicuous rudeness.

"Is Mrs. Turnbull in, do you know?"

"No idea. Sorry." This time he didn't bother to look back. It was obvious the old woman wanted to walk down with them—the last thing he wanted. But Elizabeth was persistent.

"You don't know if she's in?"

Something made the young woman hesitate. She looked back and caught sight of a desperate determination on Elizabeth's face as she hobbled to keep up with them. "I really couldn't say," she answered and then, softening a little, "Have you been to see Miss Ridgely?"

"Miss Ridgely?" Elizabeth looked fiercely blank. Her mind scrambled about in its seventy-six years' clutter looking for clues to this Ridgley person's identity. Finally the name on the sign that she had seen but not registered on her way up the drive flashed back from her subconscious like a subliminal message.

"She's not in," she said.

Longer lasting than the image of the carved name at the side of the leafy drive was the memory of the fear she had felt as she waited. For the entire thirty-five minutes—and she had counted each one, not with impatience but for something to hang on to—Elizabeth had been unable to tell herself why she was there.

The memory of the fear sparked a fresh panic, that she would not reach Mrs. Turnbull's house, and it urged Elizabeth to hobble closer to the young couple. The woman held back for her.

"Arthritis," said Elizabeth, which was true, and then, "I used to live around here," which was not untrue yet not wholly truthful either. For although she had not been back in sixteen years, there was not a step nor a stair in Mrs. Turnbull's house, not a window ledge, not a doorknob that Elizabeth would not have recognized, having lived there herself for more than twenty years.

Elizabeth had been just forty when she had cut herself loose from a husband, whom she dismissed summarily as a 'dead loss,' and bought the house at the bottom of the hill.

The house at that time had represented Elizabeth's soundly timbered independence. Small and set well back, it was sheltered by a hedge of glossy young laurel. Elizabeth particularly liked the laurel; it was a mark of sensible civilization in the midst of all the straying, rambling disorder of the country hedgerows. The house was private and yet not isolated. Its mullioned windows gave it an air of security and its creepered walls gave it charm. It answered Elizabeth's tastes as well as her needs but by far its most attractive feature was its price.

It was, as the agent said, 'competitively' listed, and for good reason. What had happened there might have remained an unfortunate personal tragedy but something in the way the police had handled the case had made headlines. As a result, the history of the house had become common knowledge. The previous owners, strangers, from the States it was said, had purchased their secluded home, moved in like lovebirds, keeping themselves to themselves, and committed a double suicide there. Rumour had it that the place had been covered in blood, the couple having first cut their wrists and then, alarmed at the sight of each other, floundered to the garage to close down the door and poison themselves with carbon monoxide.

Elizabeth, cool, practical, fiercely determined and very short of money, had not let someone else's misfortune spoil this opportunity. She paid her deposit, took out a mortgage and moved in. There was a certain amount of blood in odd places that hadn't been cleaned up properly and that she hadn't noticed when she had first walked through, but Elizabeth took a bucket and a brush to it and didn't let it bother her.

Although the laurel hedge was in sight now at the bottom of the hill, Elizabeth was suddenly frightened that the house would not be there, that it might somehow subside into the clay under the bent and bedraggled weeds of autumn. She felt that it was supremely important to stick with this nice, ordinary couple and she dredged around in her silted memory for bits and pieces that would keep them talking.

"Who lives there now?" she tried, nodding to one of the cottages through the trees.

The younger woman didn't know. Elizabeth tried again. "What about that one? That Dutch family still?"

But her fear of being left made her tone too short and sharp for the young couple; they had no answer for her.

"I used to know all these places," she said, half resentful, half defiant.

And it was true. When Elizabeth had moved in, she had set out, in her forthright and practical manner, to get to know her neighbours. She had quickly become good friends with the Turnbulls, who at the time lived at the top of the hill.

Mr. Turnbull had little to say for himself and spent most of the time after his retirement turning his compost. Mrs. Turnbull, on the other hand, was the kind of person one felt one could get close to, although in fact she would always elicit more information than she herself would volunteer.

"All these places," repeated Elizabeth and at that moment she remembered what she was doing at the house at the top of the hill. That house, with the long leafy drive, the one the woman called Miss Ridgley's, that was the Turnbulls' old house, their former home. The disturbed pool of Elizabeth's memory settled, cleared.

She had come so far—so far—to see her dear, her very dear friend, Mrs. Turnbull, had actually arrived at Mrs. Turnbull's house down there at the bottom of the hill, but then, standing at the side door of the house that was so quiet, so utterly quiet and closed, she had been overwhelmed with confusion and her mind had made a nasty U-turn, stranding her body now this year, on Mrs. Turnbull's top step while it plunged back sixteen years to the time when her friend had lived in the house at the top of the hill and the house she stood at now was her own.

Her stranded body then had stood and stared at what her mind told her was her own kitchen door. Of course there's no one in, it said, you're out aren't you? You're out to see Mrs. Turnbull, remember?

Elizabeth then had felt foolish, had stepped away from the door as if she had just come out, had slowly, had painfully, climbed the hill until she reached Mrs. Turnbull's house—old house, that is. There she had begun to repeat the whole procedure, walking to the door, reaching for the bell. And then it had come again, that terrible, unnerving confusion, like an octopus scrambling over her brain. Elizabeth knew she was wrong again. She knew she shouldn't be there.

In her embarrassment, Elizabeth, about to start out of the driveway had been scared to return. She was scared the way one would be were one to go to bed alone in a locked and darkened room and wake to the sound of breathing.

Her mind had given up on the business about houses, given up on Mrs. Turnbull and receded like a freak wave never to come back again. She no longer knew where she was or why she had come, but more troubling still she could not remember how she had come to be there at all. And so she had waited, her panic springing up like stakes in the ground around her. After a while she had calmed a little, listened to rustlings, listened to bird noises and hoped that someone would come by.

"When was that? That you lived here," asked the young woman and it sounded more like a trap than a friendly inquiry so that Elizabeth now in her turn became evasive.

"Quite a while ago, my dear. Quite a while."

But evasive answers have a way of nudging curiosity and the young woman, just as Elizabeth had done, persisted.

"Where do you live now?"

"Me? In a hotel. A hotel in town." Although she still could not remember how she came to be in this place, Elizabeth could recall the retirement home quite distinctly.

She always called it a hotel. It seemed more accurate, having none of the connotations of permanence of the word "home."

How she had come to lose it was something that still puzzled her. Her friends, her family, what there was of it, had all wanted her to move out. It was Mrs. Turnbull who had alerted them.

After Mr. Turnbull died, the widow had spent more time with her friend. It was then that she found her behaving strangely. On three separate occasions, she said, she had found Elizabeth scrubbing at the walls with a brush and a bucket of disinfectant.

Everyone knew what invisible stains Elizabeth was working at. In itself, this enfeeblement of the mind would not have been particularly harmful—or so her friends asserted to each other—but it took a more dangerous, potentially dangerous, turn when Elizabeth took to opening all the windows to let out the fumes. She would wake at night sometimes to do this. No one, least of all Mrs. Turnbull, wanted Elizabeth sleeping alone in an open house.

Despite the pressure from those who cared about her, Elizabeth would not have yielded and moved out had it not been for the argument.

One day, when Mrs. Turnbull had been suggesting that perhaps she herself should come down and sleep over for a week or two, some part of her determination and resolve that had become brittle over the lonely years, some part of her independence that had dried out like touchwood, caught fire and her anger was uncontrollable. She had rifled through her handbag, thrown the house keys at Mrs. Turnbull and taken herself off to a hotel.

Somewhere between that day and this, Elizabeth had, apparently, signed away her house. This was the part Elizabeth had difficulty talking about, not to say remembering.

One thing was certain. Mrs. Turnbull, who had begun by taking care of the house when Elizabeth had made off in such a rage, was now regarded in general and by the law in particular as its owner.

Elizabeth's progress was painfully slow. The young woman began to wonder how Elizabeth had reached Miss Ridgley's. Buses from the city didn't come out this far.

"Victoria's quite a way. Does Mrs. Turnbull know you're coming?"

"No, dear. She doesn't know." I wouldn't be in this fix, would I, thought Elizabeth, if she knew?

"Well, I think you may be in luck anyway," said the young woman. She could see a glitter of chrome through the thick laurel that screened the house.

Something like pins and needles was beginning to happen in Elizabeth's memory.

"Yes," said the young woman with satisfaction, "there's her car in the drive."

No. It's not her car. It's not her car, thought Elizabeth. She knew whose car she was going to see. The pins and needles spread and thinned, leaving behind a slippery, queasy sensation of instability, but at last Elizabeth could remember how she had left the city and come to be here.

She remembered the heart-shifting rushes of adrenaline as she took the keys of the matron's car, the sickening suspense as she sat for the first time in fifteen years behind a steering wheel. She remembered the relief as the mechanical actions and reflexes returned easily.

It could not have been more unfortunate for Elizabeth that she was not stopped. She had made a few mistakes but finally had reached the highway and slipped into the flow of traffic and it was as if the car were running itself. She was driving but she was not sure where. She knew that the sun should be behind her as she left the city and she remembered place names that sailed by but she had no thought to use them, only to drive, to keep on driving, north.

The steering wheel was slippery under Elizabeth's hands, and her eyes burned with the effort of staring straight ahead. Everything slid by in a curious, detached manner. It was all taking place on the other side of the glass, silently, and no matter how fast Elizabeth drove, she could not become part of it.

She had turned suddenly from the highway the moment she noticed the red veined alder and the stands of dark fir away over the turned fields. She had driven fiercely then, without slowing, between the scrawny hawthorn and the deep ditches, knowing exactly where to turn each time.

But although she obeyed no signs, no limits, no one had stopped her.

"There," said the young woman, relieved for Elizabeth and relieved for herself too, that she need have no further involvement. "There *is* someone home."

And there, in front of the open empty garage, was the matron's beige sedan smirking at Elizabeth, saying, "*Now* you have to drive me back."

Elizabeth stood weakly in the driveway, feeling she was going to gag and not knowing where to turn.

The young man, waiting for his wife to catch up, called out to Elizabeth, "Try the side door."

Elizabeth began obediently to shuffle away towards the side door and out of sight of the couple.

She waited until she could no longer hear the crunch of their hiking boots on the country road. The bird noises returned. She heard a squirrel scutter at the foot of a dark hemlock.

It was dark inside the garage too when Elizabeth had pulled down the corrugated steel door and it roared tremendously. And yet if you listened, if you stayed really, really still, thought Elizabeth, you could hear the other noises too.

She heard the squirrel scutter again, then the birds singing, and leaves everywhere falling, rustling, like whispers. She leaned over to open the passenger door. Mrs. Turnbull would want to sit and listen with her, when she came home.

MEMENTO

MARIA IS PACKING. SHE HAS BEEN PACKING AND UNPACKING FOR five days. Neighbours drop by from time to time to see how she is getting on. Maria has received four St. Christophers and a hand-embroidered face cloth; the villagers are not well travelled. To be truthful, the villagers are not at all travelled and the blue and white crenellations of the sunny coast are all the borders they have seen. Maria makes a point of smiling cheerily when her neighbours talk about her journey; her stomach slithers at the thought of it.

Maria is alone. It is nearly bedtime but she has to find something in the suitcase. She rummages it to the surface —a small tissue-wrapped packet, a gift, this, not for her but from her—and begins to rearrange the layers of dark, limp dresses and pale underwear. At the bottom of the case are two white towels. Maria would not think to dirty linen other than her own. This time she lays the flesh-coloured bloomers and the thick black stockings between the towels where the customs men, she is satisfied, will not have to touch them. Maria takes the packet and unwraps it. It is a medallion, a sacred souvenir for the grandchild she has never seen. The most contemporary, the most forward-looking Maria could find, this Virgin, stamped on a wafer of gold, is bionic in her perfect proportions and sports a halo of cosmic rays.

It is a gift for the child and yet not for the child. Maria hopes her godless son will be warmed by the blessings programmed into this holy chip. But Maria cannot tell herself as much.

He will know, of course, what Maria is trying to do and Maria will know, but it will make no difference, because she will still believe that it is just a gift. Maria is at once so naive and so cunning that she deceives even herself.

Despite all this, Maria longs to see this son of hers again. After all these years. After—even after—the lie he left with her, the one he whispered at his father's deathbed, mouthed. But she heard.

"No, Father, I shall not give up the Church, ever."

And already the seminary finished with him, the papers from the Vatican on their way. And already the hard-limbed foreign woman waiting for him across another continent.

Such a lie. A lie to keep Maria company all the days of her widowhood. And nights. Night after night she lay awake trying to calculate the spiritual damage of such grave deceit. But the truth worse still! He *was* giving up, had already left, the Church. Maria's spiritual account book could not register the enormity of such a transgression; it was, surely, the Unforgivable Sin.

Maria dries her eyes. She re-wraps the gift, tucks away the packet and cheers herself with visions of the child, the curly-haired cherub. There is no harm. It is a small indulgence.

She lays out her clothes for the journey, the black skirt, the white Sunday blouse. She unpins her thick, grey hair, combs it, braids it. She says her prayers.

Now her head is heavy on the pillow but, though she closes her eyes, she cannot unsee the faces. They come and go, recede, reappear; they merge one into the other, sacred and profane, a pre-Raphaelite cherub, a beauty parlour Madonna, the face of her husband, tired, fixed in a silver frame, the face of Christ pressed into a hand-towel, her son at the door of a furnace, smiling . . .

There is a place where centuries of sunshine have bleached the stone walls of the houses to the whiteness of shells, a place where the scent of wild marjoram blows on a warm wind through village streets. Here the men sit all afternoon in the shade of the fig tree, making the same conversation they made the day before over their rough, red wine. Here women whisper and laugh in cool kitchens, celebrate secrets and dismiss the simple-mindedness of men. There is little money in this place but enough food. Life is threadbare; it is accepted as such. In this place the church is heady with incense and candles burn away sins before heaven.

Maria has travelled a hundred years from here. Her son, consciously, dutifully filial, takes her by the elbow past the steel and glass and across the soundless, skidless vinyl. The automatic doors exhale and Maria, her son still lightly touching her, walks out into the fast rainshine of the bright, noisy night.

It should not have been like this. Maria dreamed it otherwise: glad faces, cheeks running with tears, mouths smiling with kisses. She dreamed a whole family at the barrier, the son, the wife, the wife's family. And the child! Oh, the child! She was clutching a small bunch of violets. But there are no flowers. There is no long embrace against warm skin, no linking of arms. There is only the son, his brief squeeze and his dry, bristly kiss.

How hard it is, Maria, not to cry. Look out into this wet Canadian night and try not to let him see. It would have helped, wouldn't it, to have had the child, held her on your lap? Tomorrow, Maria. Tomorrow they will let you see their precious. After her ten hours of carefully coddled sleep and before they send her wherever she goes to be moulded into their likeness, then you'll be allowed to touch.

It isn't much that you ask and you are patient in the waiting. Do you think he will see this, Maria?

Or will he see you dogged, determined, an old peasant

with a voracious appetite for possession? Then the linking of arms may never take place. Have you thought of that, Maria?

Two weeks have gone by and still Maria cannot really be said to have arrived. She is searching still for the children of her imagination. The grandchild is not at all the child Maria used to dream. Her small life undertaken with gravity. She goes to school, skates, dances, speaks French as well as English and plays *Frère Jacques* at the piano, all with desperate purpose. Between these pursuits there is little time to spare. Two weeks and still Maria has not presented the holy medallion.

And the other child, the son Maria loves, is nowhere to be seen. There was a long-lashed boy who cried in the dark and stole from the olive crock. Maria has not found him beneath the sufficient, failed priest.

And yet they are good to her, this son and his hard-limbed wife. This is true. They have paid her air fare. They have installed her, a temporary fixture in their charmingly sprigged and ruffled guest room. Nothing material is lacking. They have even arranged, at enormous inconvenience, long and tedious drives to which Maria submits with patience, staring from car windows at unlovely scenes of rock and cliff and observing how the hours of these foreign days are whipped away in the slipstream.

Maria cannot talk to the wife; the wife cannot talk to Maria. Husband and wife try to close the gaps with milky cups of coffee and extra Presto logs. In the evenings, seated on the chesterfield, they pose, briefly a family, before they acknowledge, as if it were a surprising thing, the presence of the huge TV. Then Maria is constrained to sit in silence and there is nothing left to do but count the minutes, the shortening string of beads she has to tell.

That they are oblivious is hard to bear. Maria would like to warn them of the passing of her life, the passing of their lives. But in this dream, this reality, there is no calling out. There is only the polite endurance of the gentle, irritating beginnings of death.

Maria sometimes feels incorporeal. There are moments when she has seen the wife staring at a chair where she has sat, as if her faded black has left a smudge. She is one of Lorca's ancient women, liable to disappear, reappear, at any moment. Tremendously inexpedient.

It is not that she has not tried. She has. She has tried in all the ways she knows to take flesh. She has baked and swept, folded laundry and looked in vain for mending, but always she has been most politely chastised.

It has occurred to Maria that even a quarrel would be preferable to this vacuous peace, but her son, though he is dry as bones, will not ignite. He has, it seems, nothing to burn, no regrets, no self-doubt.

And so, while the family sleeps, Maria shuffles in her cracked black leather slippers across the polished hardwood, prowling for comfort, for memories, signs, voices, prowling for warmth.

She hooks aside the heavy drapes and stares out at the trees—the towering, dripping firs—and she longs for the fragrant pines and the warmed earth of her hillsides.

But although there has been no reconciliation, no linking of arms or cupping of faces, Maria still hopes. She cannot know that her son is afraid, that for him she is the future, not the past. She is a reminder of the time to come when her soul, like a pigeon to the rafters, will fly home to the Church—and when he must wait, outside, alone, for his own time. *Memento mori.* And there will be no priest, no prayers of the faithful, no incense. Her son's detachment is superficially perfect and Maria knows only an emptiness as grey as the dawn she watches.

Maria is baking bread again today. Her dispassionate son smiles, really smiles. Maria's insistence on becoming corporeal is paying off.

Yesterday Maria gave the medallion to her granddaughter. Contrary to her fears—or hopes—there were no reprisals from her son. Indeed her son was not moved in any way at all to see this symbol of his relinquished church passing from his mother to his daughter.

The child, on the other hand, was deeply impressed, finding herself the owner of a piece of real gold.

The child now has come to play intently with the dough, glancing at Maria secretly to check the angle of her body, the turn of her forearms, to make her hands mirror Maria's exactly. When the bread is in the oven, the kitchen smells less antiseptic and Maria feels less strange.

She begins to snap beans crisply into a big pot fruited with garlic and olive oil.

The child leaves her dough and climbs up beside her. She talks continuously, petulant but happily so, not at all concerned that Maria cannot understand her words.

Maria holds out a bean pod and breaks it with deliberation, like a priest breaking the host. The child smiles and sets to work. She starts to sing. Maria begins to hum. They both smile a lot.

When the pot is full, Maria settles it on the stove and begins to clear up the kitchen. She comes to the child's dough. Her fingers remember how to make figures, miniature men and women standing in pairs. No figure without a partner.

Now she can hear clearly the sounds of the fiddle and the guitar, village music. She has to shade her eyes against the glare of the sun, but a breeze is rippling the buntings and flicking the ribbons. The wine glasses have already been filled for the second time and the patch of shade from the fig is exactly where it must be for the dance. There is laughter everywhere, blue and gold. Maria crooks the arms of the figures. She links them.

A wedding? A baptism? Maria hopes the child will see it for it fills her silence with the words she does not have. The child will smell the holy chrism, the thyme in flower, the smoke of cigars and the warm hay.

Footsteps sound along the hall and Maria starts. Briskly she clumps the figures into a ball, disposing neatly of the past and all that she believes offends her son.

But there is no need. He has not seen. He is busy lifting the lid of the bean pot, spooning up the broth.

HAGAR

THE SOUND OF WATER IN A DRY PLACE.
All my life I have been in a dry place. I have been a lizard skittering blindly in the dust, pincered in the fingers of a child and lifted from here to there, from there to here, while the father watches, nods. And I have not known the meaning. The dry earth has spun me round until East is West, West is East.

Now at last when I am alone, the sound of water reaches me. A comfort in a barren place.

Should a slave want, ask for more? But might not a slave expect, hope for less? To serve was all my pleasure. To comb out my lady's frail hair, to trace the kohl upon her eyes, to light the sandalwood. But it was never enough. It was "Hagar, make up the baby's bed. Hagar, give the baby suck." And all this too I would have done and willingly.

But there was no baby. Only the shaped air that my lady's arms described. But I did it, carried the piece of air around with me, clothed it, made to feed it. "No, Hagar. I said give the baby suck." And she makes me sit down on the floor of her tent and she takes out my breast and watches while the nipple stretches, yearns with the thought of the suckling. And I know she is looking at the young skin, taut and shining and she is thinking of her own breasts softened, dusty with age.

And he her husband was as bad. He took Eliezer outside one night and said, "Count the stars. Go on, count them." So Eliezer had to stay there all night until the master brought him in shivering in the dawn. "So you've counted my children," he said. "Those are my children, Eliezer. Every one of them." And he eighty-five and childless. He said God told him.

Mad both of them.

Only to serve. It was all I ever wanted and still they asked for more.

It was her doing. "Show me your hips, Hagar," she said. And my skirt was round my feet. "Turn around, Hagar." Then "Yes," and "Yes," again. And I turned and turned, twisting and trampling the skirt under my feet, closing my eyes against hers in my shame until she had had enough of looking. "Lie down, Hagar." And I made to pick up my skirt but her old foot like a vulture's claw stabbed at the cloth and held it there. "Lie down," she said. So I lay down naked and shamed on my mistress's bed.

Lying there, waiting, not knowing for what, watching the silk of the tent belly and snap, I was a lizard caught by a child's stick in a dry place with no rock to cover me. No sound of water.

And then outside the tent, a shuffling: I closed my eyes but I knew it was him. He came in and stopped at the foot of the bed and I heard him suck the air between his gums. He took a scarf and spread it over my face gently. Then he began. And the only word he said was the name of his wife, until afterwards, when he covered me with the scarf from my face. "Forgive me," he said. At the door he turned and bowed low to the ground and my tears slid into my hair.

I did not ask for that. No slave would ask, should be asked, for that. An old man rooting in her flesh to find himself a son.

But afterwards he looked kindly on me. His seed was in me, I knew, and I was not sad.

She was different. She hated me then, would not let me out of her sight, always watching in secret, chewing her freckled lips, her head shaking on her old neck. She saw me one morning returning with water. I was watching my shadow cast askance on the skin of the tents, the wind against me showing my belly. I stopped and put down the ewer and felt for the fullness. But then came the sound, a cry like a knife on a wheel. I saw the corner of her robe as she let down the door of her tent and I knew she had seen.

But I didn't ask for it, any of it. He even came to me again afterwards. When he should have stayed away. He came to my tent. "Hagar," he said, "Hagar." kneeling down to put his soft old woman's face against my belly. A shadow settled across the door of the tent. "My wrong be upon thee," she said. "Look how she plays the mistress over you now." But he denied it. "She's yours," he said. "Do what you want with her."

That was not right. When I looked at her face and I saw it set to do me harm, I ran. I ran far out towards Shur until I reached the wild place. And there in the midst of that dry and barren land I heard water splashing on the rocks. It was a fountain shining and laughing in the sun and I stopped and laid my cheek down under the small rain of it and let my tears fall in the water.

I can see it now, the shining, the light shining through the water, fractured and dashed upon the rock, the rock split a thousand ways by the light, so that when I looked up and saw the angel he seemed no more than a shower of water drops.

Then he spoke my name. "Hagar," he said and his voice was like the roaring of a cataract so that I thought I would break in pieces with the sound of it: "Hagar."

He asked me where I had come from and where I was going. He said I must go back. I wept again then and in my fear closed my eyes and again came the crashing of the cataract. He made me promises. He said God could hear my affliction. He said I would have a son. I would call him Ishmael, and his seed would be numberless.

Ishmael, my wild son, every man's hand against you, your hand against every man.

When the cataract died there was only the air shuddering with the rush of it. I opened my eyes and the angel was gone. The whole world was still.

All the way back I asked myself, could I see God's own light and live? The world was beautiful and I was alive, no matter how my mistress abused me. I would look in her eyes and think, "My children will be countless; I have seen an angel of the Lord."

Nothing mattered, only the coming of the child. He was born quick as a lamb, slippery, with limbs outflung and his eyes wide open. Ishmael.

I look deep into his eyes where the scraps of sky linger. I see twelve princes and I am happy. The master loves him, Ishmael, his seed, his first born. Smoke of that ancient fire.

And he is beautiful, my baby, downy skinned and sweet smelling, with long lashes to hold his tears and nails pink like snail shells.

"Ishmael. He heard. The sound of water in a dry place."

FAIRY TALE

THERE WAS ONCE A QUEEN WHO SAT SEWING BY HER WINDOW. And that is enough to begin, for if you know there is a queen at her window, sewing, then you know that the window frame is ebony, that outside there is snow on the ground and that small birds are shivering on the bare twigs of the trees. And there has to be blood. You know that or there is no tale. And now that we have a queen and we have blood you know too that it will be her blood and if not that then the blood of her child.

Black and white and drops of bright, bright red. There is no other way to compose this picture.

But we are still at the window, the drops of red are berries yet and the queen has not looked towards the wood.

Thus.

There was once a queen who sat sewing by her window and as she sewed sighed fondly, for she was dreaming of a child.

Now the queen was very beautiful but she lived alone in her castle, there being a certain nameless dread about her, within her, not to mention a persistent rumour that had to do with a raven, a cradle, and the day of her birth. The elements of the rumour were variable; the dread was constant.

Such was the icy nature of this dread that princes, if they gazed on her, had been known—seen, indeed—to have their eyeballs frozen in their sockets. And so none dared approach her. And who can blame them? Besides, their absence is expedient, for if a prince should enter here the blood would flow in streams or not at all, and the child when it came would be a poor thing cobbled together in haste and incomplete. But our child will be magic. This too you know or this is not a fairy tale.

So the queen was sad, counting her long years of splendid loneliness amid her tapestries, remembering the glitter of her girlhood and thinking how it had settled now into a still pool of beauty and deep, deep longing.

And, as she sewed, the queen of course pricked her finger and three drops of bright, bright blood spotted the linen and she smiled, for she knew as well as you or I that it takes only blood and a small piece of one's heart to make a child.

And so she closed her eyes and let her heart crack just a little while the drops of blood bloomed like roses on the linen.

When the queen looked up again, there was the child hurrying in a flurry of snow towards the castle in the darkness of the dusk-filling wood.

At once she knew more joy than in her whole life before and she ran outside laughing, holding her arms angel-wide. And as she bent to gather the child to her she saw that it was a dark-haired boy and her tears fell on his face.

Now the child, it hardly needs saying, was as perfect as it was inevitable. From his hair that gleamed like midnight to his skin that shone like snow, he was beautiful. Never did he lay his hand to a wicked act and never in his heart did he hold for the queen anything but love.

And yet the queen could not be happy (and didn't you suspect this all along?) for, while her love for the child was as strong as the wind, the dread that was within her began to grow, tendrilled and fast-rooted: *what if?*

It was as if a very crow upon the castle wall had spoken the words. They were clear to the queen, were near, as a footfall in the forest is near to a traveller walking alone.

Which is exactly the trouble with wishes: from *"I wish"* to *"what if"* is no distance at all; they are two sides of the same mirror. Tasting the fruit of her own power, the queen found it, not a little like knowledge, very bitter.

The queen reasoned thus: had she been able merely with a wish, a spider's thread of longing, to draw the child hurrying in a flurry of snow from the dark heart of the wood, then might she be able equally, on the merest filament of fear, to lose him.

The queen ceased to be happy. She resumed her sewing.

Always she would watch the child as it played and always she would guard her thoughts with care, leaving her fears unformed lest a spoken dread should, like a spoken wish, prove true.

Still the child grew more blessed and every day the queen's love, mingled with her dread, became a greater burden. Stark awake she lay at night for fear of dreaming harm. That she should one day be the cause of the boy's destruction was too much for her to bear.

At last, as the year turned full circle, she called her huntsman to her.

"Huntsman," she said, "there is a soul that longs to be free. Slay the creature that holds this soul a captive. Do it this kindness, for you are a good man and strong. There is no need to fear; rather would it be a wicked thing to deny a soul in need."

But the poor huntsman protested and said his will would surely fail were he to look upon the life he had to take.

So with a glance the queen took from him his sight, saying she would bring the creature in and it would lead him to a place of its own choosing to do the deed.

Then the queen left him blinded there and went to her child.

"Child," said she, "when you next see the huntsman, take what he has to offer you and think not ill of me that I love you too well." And the child, being but a child thought nothing of these words but went again to his play.

The queen then took a small box of juniper wood, returned to the waiting huntsman and in silence took his hand.

When they reached the deep of the forest she stopped and placed the box of juniper wood at his feet and then she drew his knife and placed it in his hands.

And so the huntsman took the life of the queen there in the deep of the wood with his soul frozen by her chill power and his eyes blinded by her own. But when the queen fell dead and he saw what he had done, he was indeed afraid.

The queen lay pale on the cold ground and beside her was the juniper box spilled open with its twenty golden guineas burning in the snow. In her hand was a letter with his name upon it.

The huntsman began to wish he were blind again.

Trembling he read: *"Cut out my heart and take it to the child. Do thou this thing lest the child die and my soul curse you forever."*

So he cut out the queen's heart and placed it in the box. Then he laid her body in a drift of snow and covered it from the sight of heaven.

Now this huntsman, who was merely male and frail and quite unable to cope with fairy tale, was most afraid, and on his way back he buried the heart deep in a hollow tree. Then, finding a linnet frozen upon a bare dead bough, he put it in the box and carried it away to the castle.

The child danced with joy when he saw the huntsman entering the castle gate. He remembered the queen's words and called out gaily.

"Huntsman! Huntsman! What have you for me?"

"A message from the queen," replied the huntsman. "She is gone on a long journey but she bids you know that her heart is always yours."

"And what does she send me?" cried the child.

"A gift," said the huntsman and his eyes filled with

pity, not for what he had done but for that all he had to give the hapless child was a poor dead bird.

Yet when the child opened the box out flew the linnet, singing into the clear winter air.

For many days the child was content to play within the castle walls, amused by the lovely song of the bird at his side. But he soon grew pale and sad and looked always outside the walls to the snowy wood. And now the huntsman—who was, as you have seen, quite unfortified by faerie—felt his heart fail within him and coming to the boy he knelt before him and offered him his sword.

"Kill me," he said, "for I have done a wicked thing and deserve to die."

The child of course would not touch the sword but begged to know what terrible thing the huntsman had done. But no matter how he begged or entreated he could not induce him to say another word.

At last, in tears, the huntsman rose and led the boy to the deep of the wood.

The snow was falling gently through the bare branches and there was silence on every side. Nothing stirred except the huntsman and the boy and above them the linnet, flying for all the world as if the snow were nothing more than petals tumbling from a summer tree.

In a little while they came upon the drift of snow and the boy looked upon the queen and the heart-shaped wound in her side. He cried with pity to see her so alone and cold and empty and would not come away and leave her so.

At last he rose and took the linnet from the branch where it sat and placed it where his mother's heart should be. Then he covered the place with snow and rose to go.

And as he did so—but it hardly needs telling; there is no death in faerie or, if there is, it is a small thing—a missed beat of wings in the breast. You know the rest.

The queen opened her eyes.

But the deception, the chicanery! Not only has she played false with death but the ugly dread, that too, is gone, melted magically and no clue left us, nothing to help us shift our own chill blocks, huntsmen's knives and linnets being not at our disposal.

Still we must be happy for her. She laughed with joy to see her child with the huntsman at her side and knew not at all how they came to be there all three within the dusk-filling wood. She knew only that the world had never been more beautiful or full of love. And so she let them lead her home, and wondered what she must have dreamed to bring about such joy.

Thus all her years, which were the number of a linnet's feathers, the queen lived in her castle and loved all heaven's creatures, as now she loved the boy, with the same unfearing love.

The child was happy and grew up to conjure all that he desired from the darkness of the wood. And the huntsman, the poor mortal huntsman, learned to forget, almost, all that had happened. He continued to serve the queen, though never was quite at ease, but wondered always when next he might find his eyeballs frozen in his head—at the very least.

And the heart? Yes, you have to ask about the heart but it can stay buried, bloodied in a hollow tree, or this is not a fairy tale.

SAMSON'S WIFE

BUT HOW HE WHISPERED.
So strong a man to whisper low, sweet. How I melted for him like honey in the sun.
He came down from the camp of Dan and I should have known. Striding like a lion he came down and walked into Timnath and I should have known there would be blood on his hands and honey on his lips.
I was at the well and my sister there too when he came, eyes dark flames in a field of gold corn. Then it was as if the breath of God had stopped. My sister with her hand on the pitcher to raise it. The water falling in strings from the muzzle of the ass as it lifted its head from the trough. The buzzards overhead in a circle, in a circle. And silence. The millstone across the square thundering into silence.
His white teeth.
He spoke and then from the women, such a smiling and turning away, jangle of arms across faces, sudden interest of fingers in tassels, scraping of feet at the dust. A confusion of birds at the sound of the jackal.
"Here," I said and I held up my cup to him. "Drink."
He looked into my eyes. Cup after cup he drank as if

he were saying "More. I'll take more. I'll take it all." Cup after cup until the others had gone and only my sister remained. And I. I could not look at him sitting there on the stone wall, smiling, the back of his hand across his mouth, grinning, his tongue licking his lips. His teeth. Oh, we pleased him.

After that I went every day to the well. I knew he would come again and he did. From the well he walked with me to the door of my father's house. We talked, his eyes burning mine so that I could not stay.

I made to go and he reached out but he did not touch me. There was blood on his hand. It had dried under his nails. It had settled in the creases of his fingers, laced his knuckles. The lines of his palm, were traced with it.

"Stay," he whispered. His voice so sweet, so soft. "Stay. I shall be back for you. My wife." I took his hand in both of mine, turned it and put my mouth on the dark lines on his palm. And they tasted like iron.

The next time, it was arranged. He came with his father and mother from Dan. They came with their mouths turned down and their nostrils wide, snuffing the air for Philistine dirt. But they came, with servants bringing gifts so that everyone might see, the sacks of soft flour clouding the backs of the mules, the tufted kids, the wine skins rolling heavy. They nodded, they barely smiled, but as they passed and made their way into the house he pulled me aside to the shadow of the doorway and put his mouth on mine. And honey was on his lips.

How our fathers balked like mules at the match, but it was done, settled, and the day of the feast fixed.

Now came the thirty young men. Pride of Timnath. All swagger and strut, brash with their cocksure eyes and their easy shoulders. Companions for my foreign bridegroom at the feast. All laughter and tossing heads, outdrinking the drinker, outbragging the braggart, outroaring the lion. He watched.

"Listen," he said, expansive, bold. Open-palmed. "You tell me," and the flesh over their clenched teeth flickered, "you tell me the answer to the riddle I pose and I'll give you—give you, yours to keep—one garment for each man. And a blanket—yes, a blanket, too. Thirty garments and thirty blankets if you can tell me the answer by the end of the seven days of this feast. And thirty garments, thirty blankets for me if you can't."

Then the banter, laughter into the night. He came to me only at dawn.

In the morning there was no more laughter, only bad-tempered hectoring and squabbling, like hens in a coop.

Out of the eater came forth meat.
Out of the strong came forth sweetness.

Not one of them could give him an answer.

Each day for seven days the same. Sometimes one of the young men would come to me secretly, whisperingly. Then the pleadings, cajolings in dark corners, and promises slipped like kisses into my ear. *Come, please. Tell me. Tell me and I'll give you anything you want.* But I knew nothing and I could not tell.

At night I went to him weeping, said, "Husband, you bring down my countrymen to pecking hens. You keep your secret from me. You cannot love me."

"Love you?" he said.

Honey dripped from our lips, from our fingers.

At last on the seventh day with my husband still sleeping, his mouth in a smile, three of them came to me with a firebrand.

"You think we are playing a game?" they said and pulled the veil from my head and held it to the brand so that it cringed and flared blue and green. "You," they said. "This is you and your father's house if you do not tell us before the sun goes down tonight."

Samson slept in the sun, soft like a child and his lips parted. I bent to him, my hair its own veil, shading his face.

"Come inside," I whispered, "Come in to your wife."

And there in the dark cool of my chamber while all the feasters slept off their revels we tasted the sweetness. And he told me. How he tore apart the lion with his hands. How the bees swarmed from heaven and made honey in the carcass.

What good to say I should have known? I knew always. It was traced in the lines on his palm. And all the sweet tears of our loving were wept for what was to come. What is left to say? I told him his secret, they completed the riddle, he was mad with rage.

That night he left the feast and went down to Ashkelon. He went in to our neighbours, our friends asleep, and returned, leading two mules. On the backs of the mules thirty garments, thirty blankets, and all of them bloodied.

How the fire spreads! Gold honey melting in the hot sun, running in all directions as if the flames are the tails of foxes racing through the standing corn, brushing it alight, while in the next field the cut sheaves, blackened, crumble and fall in. How it runs abroad, sending tongues ahead of itself, licking up the gold. Above it the smoke darkening the blue with the smell of danger.

The men cannot beat it back. The corn gone, the fire tears past them, between them, and it is in the vineyards, the olive grove. Now the air crackles with the sound of the men's voices breaking.

Why did he return? Did he think I would wait here, the good wife, after he left on the seventh day? After he went back to Dan, to his own people? Leaving us with the heaps of cloth, heavy and dark, staining the floor of my father's house.

Father was kind and did what he could for me in my shame.

"I'll find you a new husband," he said. "To look after you." Now I live here in my father's house, the wife of my husband's best man.

Should I have known he would return? Did I know? Always? How he would come back at harvest, the same man my husband, who killed the sleeping villagers, and stand at the door, humble, holding the white kid soft as a dove in both his hands, an offering?

From my chamber I listened.

"No you cannot come in. She is taken."

"Taken?"

"But you hated her utterly. She is given to your friend for a wife."

Such a silence. Like a millstone in pieces.

"You may take her sister. See how beautiful."

And still the silence, until the sound of the kid bleating as he walked away.

His rage burns up our land, consumes the stored sweetness. The vineyard is in flame and beyond it the olive trees roar as they burn.

The exhausted men have put down their beaters. They are kindling brands in the smouldering field.

Retribution. And no one to pay it but me.

ONLY YESTERDAY

PHYLLIDA WILD AND RECKLESS AND NOT TO BE TAMED.
    Phyllida slim and dark, black hair caught up behind in a soft dense mass. When she smiles her eyes flash dark wings. But Phyllida loves sun. Come with me, she says. We shall fly in the sunlight.
    She'll come to no good, they said.
    They said this and loved her anyway. No good. Because she flashed darkness. So Phyllida grew and the young men came, shy, afraid of the smile and the dark wings but wanting. Oh, wanting. And she enjoyed their clumsy courtship, their blunderings where they should not go, their stammering kisses and the stutter of the heart.
    Sometimes Phyllida and the young men would ride in motor cars along the apple-scented lanes and she would pull her hat down tight around her ears and narrow her eyes against the whipping breeze.
    Barney had a motor bike and this was bliss. It tore along beside the hedgerows. It shattered the sweet buzz and chatter of the summer air, snarled its way down into drowsy villages and roared its way out of them. Phyllida learned to sit just so, and then just so in the sidecar to take

it faster through the curves. Phyllida in goggles. Coming to no good. And then she learned to ride it.

The young men watched and bit the inside of their cheeks and ribbed her bravely. Sometimes she rewarded one of them. This one, the favoured one, would dress lengthily, attentively, utter a curse or two for Barney, and take a deep breath before he knocked at the door. Then, because Phyllida was Phyllida, he thought her really his and his legs became jointless, rubber, and his heart jumped up behind his shirt front every time she smiled.

But Barney said he had a problem with his machine and could not get about without her. So she rode always with him, leaning precariously from the sidecar to pour her teapot full of petrol into the carburetor.

Phyllida wild.

It was not long before they said more. She dances, yes. Without shoes. And that's not the half of it. Climbed the water tower and Alfred Barnes went up there too. Behind her. She needs a talking to, she does.

Phyllida put the wicker picnic basket under the hedge and lay down with Jed at the edge of the cornfield. The breeze stroked the yellow corn and it rustled. Poppies blinked in its waves. The white goat on the other side of the hedge reached forward with her tight lips to catch up the blue ribbons of Phyllida's straw hat where Jed had thrown it in the hawthorn. The new straw snagged on the branches as the goat tugged it through.

Phyllida and Jed lay on their sides with their foreheads touching, their eyes not seeing while Jed held her by the hair and said, "Don't," and again, "Don't, Phyllida. Don't marry him."

Because they wanted the sadness not to end, they lay together, just touching, barely. When they got up and banged the dust out of their clothes, the goat had finished the brim and was halfway through the crown, chewing up their sadness, remorseless.

Phyllida and Jed lay down a while longer, happy. Then

they drank their ginger ale, gave their sandwiches to the goat and went home. Phyllida hatless. Jed with a blue ribbon in his pocket.

So Phyllida married Barney, and the young men looked rueful, then wry, as they remembered their times with her and then it was wartime and they forgot.

Barnes joined the Royal Engineers and spent the war lying under trucks in parts of Europe. He was a wizard with machines.

Phyllida went to work in an explosives plant and it exploded. Everyone thanked God that Alfred Barnes was far away, overseas. She lay on her side in the hospital bed for three months, the skin and hair of the left half of her body slowly healing, slowly renewing.

And then she could sit up and look around and her eyes stuck open on the things she saw and she was never quite the same—though people, not having seen the things she saw, the curtains of the other beds drawn discreetly at visiting time, said always it was the blast that changed her.

She stayed close to her father after that, as if his big hands could shield her from the things she continued to see. People said it was a crime. Someone ought to see about her. She should get out a bit.

When Phyllida went back to work at the factory, the scars on her face were watermarks only and the plant was making something new. No one thought the war would last so long. It seemed like only yesterday.

And then it was over.

Barney and the young men, some of them, returned. For a while Barney tried to make it all the same, but William and Mac were dead and Jed was married somewhere in France and Phyllida, when the young men were near, would only sit with her left hand up to the side of her face, just touching, barely. And friends moved away. It was not the same.

Alfred Barnes began to build a workshop, glazed on the roof and on one side like a conservatory. When it was finished he did not need the old friends. He filled the workshop with black machinery and oil-smelling parts. Other men came now. They cupped greasy nests of cast iron tenderly in their palms and nodded their approval. Sometimes they nodded to Phyllida as she passed them in the hallway and they coughed, but out of courtesy only, and Barney did not introduce them.

The smell of grease oozed into the house under the workshop door. It larded the meat and the puddings in the pantry. The geraniums on the window sill seemed to shrink. Phyllida put them outside early.

Phyllida stood at her kitchen sink and stared across the fields that fell away gently from the house and swelled again to the horizon. A tractor crawled across the far side. Seagulls and crows tumbled in the air behind it. Down at Mattock's farm the plum trees were extravagant with fleece. There would be bluebells in the shade.

Alfred was cutting something. The screaming of the metal made Phyllida's teeth ache. She left the dishes and went outside. The scream diminished to a drone. She sat on the warm brick path. After a while the drone stopped. She pulled some weeds and turned a little plot where she thought to put in peas and then she went inside to see if Alfred—she had taken to calling him Alfred—was ready for his dinner. But he had gone. The stove was out and there was a film of black machine oil over the dishes in the sink.

When Alfred came back he was music-hall drunk.

That night she sat up late in the kitchen with the stove popping and the clock keeping its wooden time on the mantle. Then she went and lay down beside her snoring, reeking husband. Phyllida coming to no good.

The house seemed cold after that and Phyllida stayed outside in the sunshine. Alfred would work a little and then go out again.

There was no talking about this thing. It had come like a sudden draught under a door, like a fall of soot in the chimney. It became the pattern of their days, sometimes better, sometimes worse, for Alfred did not always contain his drunken anger.

There were some who said that Alfred Barnes hit his wife. But Phyllida spoke to no one of these things, told no one that he hit her once, hard, and that the second time he tried she took the poker to his head and split his ear. Alfred had to be careful in that workshop of his, the doctor said, those machines were dangerous.

There were no children. Though Phyllida could still flash darkness from her eyes, Barnes was after glitter and he went into the town for that. People talked, but in the end said little. Barney always was a lad.

Because she spoke to no one and left this sore alone, Phyllida's sadness turned to resignation, her resignation to content. Alfred came and went as he pleased, leaving greasy thumb prints and the smell of iron in his track. Phyllida slipped away easily from his approach and kept to her garden, hacking at first and digging fiercely, but before long tending it with care.

In the chill days she piled on woollens and worked until her nose ran and her fingers ached and only when the last of her plants had blackened and broken down for the winter did she come in and sit in her kitchen. In these winter evenings she would sit before the open door of the stove, sit and rock, sit and rub the chilblains on her ankles, sit and sit. Phyllida tamed.

In spring Phyllida bought hens from Mattock's and built a coop away from the noise of the machines. Cats appeared and slept their days away on the warm stones outside the kitchen window or curled like fur hats on the vacant chairs in the empty parlour.

Phyllida's garden grew green and generous, purposeful, the cabbages so dense and solid they crushed the weeds beneath them. The scarlet runners wove a high and tangled screen, a tapestry of tendrils and flowers. The very potatoes seemed to knock together beneath the heaved earth. And among the flowers, the Canterbury bells and larkspur, the cornflowers and the cinnamon-scented wallflower, among these moved Phyllida, intent as any bee.

When Phyllida, to take her ease, wandered down beyond the hen coop to the unkempt patch beside the hedge of sloes and old-man's beard, she would pick the wild flowers. In April the ground under the hedge was smoked with bluebells. In June there were poppies.

The settled years continued and Phyllida came to want nothing more. She knew every leaf and flower, every bud and shoot in her garden and it was enough. In its way. Phyllida happy.

Visitors still would call and she would come, mud-spotted, wind-blown, in from the garden to greet her Sunday-dressed callers and seat them in the cold parlour. When they talked she would listen and be happy for them, for their new motor cars, their foreign travel, their clever children. When Phyllida talked, which was not often, she had nothing to tell—the budding of the lilac not being news but only to be expected—and her visitors would notice the earth under her nails, the dust on the china plates, the soot in the unlit hearth. Sometimes they would talk about the old days and Phyllida would flash her smile and they would feel as if, by some power of their own, they had conjured the past out of a hat, alive and springing against the present air. But afterwards the room seemed colder still.

They said she had no kind of life, sitting there day in, day out. Bitter, she was. Always dwelling on the past. Only to be expected, they said. In the circumstances.

Phyllida old. Brown and wrinkled as her tobacco, body bent and reaching to the earth. Phyllida tough and generous as her tangling brambles. No bitter berries.

Phyllida in her apron and her slippers sat outside on the step and watched long streamers of white smoke uncurl from the burning stubble and drift low across the hill. There was no noise from the lathe in the workshop and the air was very quiet, very light. The two cats rolled in the dust at her feet. She thought about children. Sometimes now she allowed herself to think about children.

Inside, Alfred wandered unbuttoned from room to room, looking for something—he could not remember what. The doctors had said his stroke was mild, that he would get his senses back. But he never did. Although he walked and ate and slept and drank, that too, as ever, he could not work. And so he was at large, unpredictable and menacing as one of his machines worked loose from its bearings and come rocking into the house.

Phyllida picked up her cup and went inside. It was quiet. Her heart stuttered hard. But Alfred was only sleeping.

For many years Alfred cheated death and in that time Phyllida grew thinner still. People talked but it was all surmise for Phyllida did not choose, would never have chosen, to betray Alfred and his indignities. She was patient, and Alfred, when he had had enough, died.

In the quiet of the house Phyllida thought she could hear the whine of the machines and smell the acrid smoke of the torch. She had a dealer come and cart away the innards of the workshop. People said she was a fool, that it was worth a fortune. Phyllida reckless.

She found the whitewash and the step-ladder and set to work, climbing the rickety steps, teetering and puffing and making her heart jabber, but with excitement now, as whiteness bloomed over the blackened back wall and spattered the floor with its petals. She filled the bench with plants and set a table and chair in the centre of the room so that she might sit there on bright winter days and watch cloud shadows flash darkness on the downs. And this was bliss.

Phyllida hoped to die in this room and be found as one might come upon a spider in an empty house, dried up in its web in the corner of a sunny window. But Phyllida had years yet to live.

Each year the tall grasses and brambles gained a little ground and each year the garden rambled closer to the house to fling its vines and creepers against the walls and show its wild beauty at the glass of the whitewashed room.

Phyllida wizened now and brittle, with skin like paper and bones like sticks. She has her bed moved into the whitewashed room and sleeps with a paraffin fire burning all night, the stove in the kitchen not quite heating the empty house.

People say she is a danger. Something should be done. She's not all there. Phyllida shuffles through her days, caring for herself, a little, and sleeping. The house is always cold. It takes her long to dress. There are layers and layers of woollen clothes, of socks, of mittens. It is easier not to take them off. It's not right, people say.

And people come often now. Phyllida is suspicious of this sudden attention until it comes to her, like a bright idea in the night, that they are calling to see if she is still alive. This idea awakens her interest. She stays alive in order to greet them when they call. Cat and mouse.

The day is high and wild, a day when clouds scud and rooks hurtle in the blue sky. Every tree and bush is rimmed with bright new green, alive with it. The morning is a kaleidoscope of light. It glints from the flowerpot roofs of the new bungalows over on the downs. It glances from the tractors down at Mattock's, dashes from the fence tops and shivers in the cats' fur.

Phyllida sits in the sunshine sheltered by the bright glass. Her feet, inside their socks, inside their slippers, are wrapped in woollen scarves to warm them. She sits in her chair and a young man sits on the edge of the bed.

He is talking to her but she cannot remember who he is. A nephew? He is talking about his bike, a motorbike. Phyllida has a vacant look and the young man remembers what they say. And indeed Phyllida is not all there but in another place entirely. She blinks against a whipping wind and the young man watches her eyelids elaborate their folds. And then she smiles and behind her eyes is a beating of wings against the wind, a sudden shadow, warmer than sunlight.

SITTING PRETTY

SHE FELT COMFORTABLE SITTING THERE, SUPREMELY comfortable. It was the comfort of release, as when a pain is eased, a whine silenced, an itch scratched, a thirty-six-hour girdle peeled stickily away from its compressed contents. She was luxuriously at rest.

It was her weight.

For years she had hauled it up and down stairs, heaved it into supermarkets and then stuffed it into and dumped it out of buses, all in the course of her labours in an unlikely and unrewarding alliance. But at last she was letting it do exactly as it wanted. It made her seem, for the time that she sat there, weightless. It was as if her whole being had dropped, plumb-like into the vast, cushiony depths of her buttocks, accommodating, commodious hassocks that they were, to swallow at a go her whole cumbersome, bothersome bulk.

As a result her head floated detached and smiling serenely above the empty, porridge-blotted pinafore, and in like manner her feet, they too, almost smiled below.

Harbingers of trouble her feet were—and ever had been. When they were bad, taut and shiny and itchy with old chilblains, it always meant she had been standing too long at the sink or the ironing board and that, in its turn, meant that he had stayed too long at the pub and would return with cheeks veined and purpled to match her ankles.

Her feet being such sore points, as it were, it was heartening to see them happy. And she *could* see them nestled there side by side on his waistcoat, overflowing the edges of their worn slippers like jumbo pork sausages escaping from their skins.

She could see them for she had drawn them in, bending her knees and letting her legs fall wide. She couldn't remember having been in such a position since their camping holiday, when the Porta-Jon was blocked and she had had to find a place in the bush.

Only last week she had seen an article called 'Posture Points' in one of her weeklies. There were comic strip figures in right and wrong poses showing how to 'look inches taller', 'diminish unsightly rolls' and 'minimize chubby knees.' She wondered how many posture points she would lose for this one.

There really were only three positions she used of late. There was lying, like a downed dirigible, there was standing —the whole trouble with her puffed feet—and there was sitting, or, more accurately, seated, always on something and always with her body articulated in the likeness of an armchair.

This was different.

Of course if he was around—well, he *was* around but never mind—she would never have been able to let herself go like this. Cruel he was. She often used to wonder why he didn't go on the road and do the bars with his fat lady jokes. *Got a modelling job, my wife has, posing for Save-the-Whale. No, lovely lady, my wife. Got picked up by the coast guard. Took her for an inflatable life-raft.* Nasty little mind. That's what he should have done, she thought. Gone and made some money with it. She wouldn't have minded. Not if he'd sent her half. Gone to live in Florida she would have. Where Doris went. Worn bikinis, too. (*How many, dear?*)

She'd have looked all right brown. At least she was all smooth. Not lumpy like some fat people. Carriage, too, she had. (*More like undercarriage.*) And a nice face when she had her hair done. People with money had their hair done every day if they wanted. Someone to do it for them. A little higher at the back, ducks. Lovely! Someone to do everything for them.

The thought of it.

Oh, she'd have been all right if they'd had money. If he hadn't drunk it all. The sponge. The weedy sponge. He never did tell her how much he made. Well, she'd soon find out.

What a fool she'd been. All these years working and never seeing anything, not a glimmer, of her own money, let alone his. Trotting round every Friday like a trained poodle straight from payroll to the supermarket. She might as well have been paid in tea and butter. (*How about lard, dear?*) *Rump steak,* she answered and settled down savagely.

She was getting angry again. It was too much, hearing his smirky remarks, his wheezy old croak again, even if it was all inside her head. She had put an end to it and that ought to be enough. The little squirt.

She shifted her weight and thought for a moment that she saw his foot twitch. It was obscenely exciting to think it might have.

She shifted again, just slightly, but there was nothing, and she decided it must have been a reflex. Like ants' legs. They do that.

Yes, it was a good likeness. Definitely an ant, mouth like a set of beaky little pinching jaws, skin like armour plate. Or a flea. Press it under your thumb and it jumps away good as new.

The only time she had ever got to him had been once early on. She couldn't even remember what it was about now but by God he'd been mad. Came at her with a broom, he did. A broom! And she'd been so amazed she had just stood there like a dumb animal while he did it.

All that afternoon she had cried but not for the bruises. She had cried the way she had as a child when she had seen the cow get its leg stuck in the ramp at the market, with everyone poking and shoving and yelling at it and her not knowing why. She didn't cry these days, not in front of him, but she couldn't help trying to get to him still, even if it was no use. 'Look what you're doing to me! Look at the state of me! Can't you see?'

Even after the last time, when she knew he'd been having a bit with that tight-lipped, tarty Simpson woman, even then he'd had nothing to say. 'Take it easy, dear. You're upset. Take the weight off your feet.' He was always saying that. It was the only thing his pea brain could ever come up with. *Sit down, dear. Take the weight off your feet.*

Well, here I am. Dear.

No, she shouldn't feel guilty about it. He had it coming all right—

Coming as it did from beneath her, the sound made her jump in a paroxysm of embarrassment. But when she realized that she had just heard the last earthly sound he was ever to make, the rush of hot colour that washed over her body was one of pleasure rather than fright.

She waited.

Slowly, slowly the wash of heat subsided and in an orgasm of relief she smiled.

No, there was no feeling guilty. Twenty years is enough of feeding a sneering face that has nothing but bad jokes and beery breath to offer. It had been about time it got what it deserved. And tonight, when he walked in with his silly grin, simpering *(You shouldn't have waited up, dear. Don't want to miss your beauty sleep.)*, when he went on through to the back and relieved himself on her nasturtiums *(Not on your what?)*, when he came back in, upsetting the cat box *(Put the damn broom down, will you. You can do it in the morning.)*, picked up the rhubarb crisp she had saved for his dinner and dropped it (*Tits!*), then it did indeed begin to be time.

Whether he meant to clear up the mess was never quite clear to her, but when he spoke about the broom, the damn broom again, and started to reach for it, then it was more than time.

She had hurled herself at him as he came at her, knocking him backwards into the cat litter and sinking her knees and her two hundred and eighty pounds into his chest. Then, with the grace and speed of an all-in wrestler, she had switched her position, turning one hundred and eighty degrees and holding him all the while beneath her so that his startled, pop-eyed, gape-mouthed face could take in the fundamental ponderability of its fate, the gravity of it, as her buttocks came floating down like twin, lead-weighted parachutes settling to earth.

So here she was, still in this ungainly (was it lewd?) position, too happy to move.

Heavy and weightless at the same time. Free. If he could see her . . . But of course he couldn't. Not unless he had his eyes open. And even if he had . . .

Her mind blushed at the thought but she settled herself more comfortably—and it felt delicious.

FACES

NOREEN IN THE ALMOST DARK BITES HER NAILS. SHE NIBBLES at the quick where the hangnails weep and her teeth know just how much before the hurt. It is a careful calculation. Noreen bites her nails when she has to think and now she must think harder than she has ever needed.

Downstairs her mother is talking about this year's crop of Coxes and how the frost has done them good. Her brother is reading the paper while he eats. "Yeah," he says, as if this were a night like any other. "Yeah," so that she can hear the crisp flesh break, making her own mouth water for sweetness or perhaps for sadness.

How Noreen wishes not to have to think. For when she has thought she must speak. Or not. So intolerable is the outcome of either that she is immobilized. Her mind refuses to engage despite the workings of her teeth. There is only the question, as immovable as a wall. To tell?

"No use for cooking, but they'll keep. If we're careful."

She hears their voices plainly and they seem to her to bear all innocence within the burly words that are, impossibly without blight, rolling off their tongues.

"Best crop that tree's seen."

"That's what your dad said." And there it is, one bite too many. There is a small silence as Noreen's mother considers what to do with this mouthful of worm. For her husband is out and will not be back until it is done. If he is lucky. And this they all know, only accommodate differently. She decides to swallow.

"Well," she says. "Can't sit here all night." Getting up. Knowing, from years of it, how to close the door on the uninvited, how to fold the piece of dirty linen in with the clean.

Noreen's brother says "No." But still he sits, reliving terrors of his own: the time he had to go back, retrieve the plant "for political reasons," the time they had picked him up right after. Times he had emptied his bowels so fast it burned. But that wouldn't stop him and if he only had the chance—for his foot is half shot away and he is no bloody use, he knows—he would be there tonight alongside his father giving the bastards their one all-fucking-mighty birthday surprise.

"Holy Mary, mother of God," Noreen prays but the rest of the words will not come, a flight of angels with wings resolutely folded. "Help me," she says instead. Seeing her father at his work, his hands, big as they are, quick and certain, the detonator in them as easy and comfortable as a packet of cigarettes, the copper wires obedient. He could be a woman sewing, so sure he is, and relaxed. Threading his slow fuse, sewing a live circuit into the dark.

Noreen sits bolt upright on the edge of her bed and her teeth clatter like bones. Never mind Our Lady. She knows without being told.

And yet. Her own father.

She is a child again, watching his broad back as he reaches into the hutch, brings out the one he has chosen, his hands gentle and he not dreaming to be otherwise even as he takes it behind the shed. She can see the rabbit soft and heavy on his forearm, one of its hind feet paddling air as it searches for the warm platform of his hand.

Betray him for a bloody British soldier?

But even as she draws up her knees with the pain of it she knows she will, though there is no helping the soldier now. Who died while she watched outside the pub, the side of his face pushed against the step. She saw it, there was no turning away. He looked right at her as he died, the bloody British soldier, looked right into her, his eyes saying help me and his mouth, on some last convulsion, curling at the lip, opening with the pressure of the unbearable, the unvoiced pleading, and the expression on him the same as the boy under the bridge by the school, that first one who kissed her and looked as if he might die with the wanting, so that she had to answer yes with her own eyes yes, even though it was a lie and he was dead perhaps even before he saw it.

She knows now that against these faces, these private agonies of both the living and the dead, all the years of struggle and oppression are nothing, not her father's fight, not even the risk of his being taken. And she knows that she will do it.

But first she must tell herself lies.

She tells herself that her father will not be in any danger, that he is too clever, that if she is careful there will be plenty of time, he will get clean away. She says no one need ever know who made the call. She says if they ever come looking it will make no difference, she can swear that black is white. He never left the house.

When she has finished, her mind is numb and she lies down on the bed to stare into the darkness past the chimneys and wait for this night to pass.

Her brother, sprawled on the settee in front of the TV he isn't watching, under the splayed edges of a newspaper he isn't reading, calls to their mother in the kitchen.

"You're gonna miss the beginning."

Noreen hears the living room door close.

Voices break out into the street when the pub down the road empties; as they grow more distant they take with them that part of her that listened, and she feels smaller, lonelier. The traffic thins and she begins to doze, conscious of doors closing, locks turning downstairs, the taps . . .

It is important to make the call at exactly the right time. Too early and the whole country will be studded with roadblocks to trap him coming back.

She wakes with a start and realizes that it is too late. She is already wearing her track suit; her trainers are beside the bed ready. She puts them on and ties them, her fingers snagging in the knowledge of this lateness. She treads the stairs as if they might crack under her weight, thinks she hears her brother rouse anyway. But there is no turning back. I couldn't sleep, she'll say. I needed some exercise.

It is still dark. The road is deserted. She hears the whine of the milk van two roads away. She can even hear the soft fizz of its tires on the wet surface.

When she reaches the phone box she has to stop herself from turning to look over her shoulder. Nice and normal, Noreen. What her mother said when she rehearsed her bridesmaid's mincing walk behind her cousin with the yellow hair.

Nice and normal.

Nine, nine, nine.

"Please," she says after she has asked for the police. Be nice. She has to hold the receiver with two hands. Normal.

"Don't let the bus leave the barracks. It's wired." But her voice is a whisper.

"Don't let the bus leave the barracks." She repeats it louder. She will wake the street but still they can't seem to hear her.

"Don't—" Then it dawns on her and she puts the phone down fast.

She would like to run back now, like a rabbit to cover, but she continues on round, rehearsing. I needed some air.

"Where've you bin?"

Her brother is sitting at the kitchen table with the radio on. He looks around, staring over his shoulder as she goes upstairs.

"Out." The small word an inadequate disguise.

"At this hour?"

"It's a free country."

In her room the shaking becomes intolerable. It has travelled from her hands to her arms and now her legs too begin to dance. She sits down and folds her arms tight around her stomach as if she is in pain, wrapping her legs around each other. The furniture in the room jigs in front of her eyes.

If her brother or her mother should come in now she is finished. She closes her eyes and sees her father's face as she saw it when they told him about her brother, the muscles under the eyes bunched for protection, the top lip drawn up in disbelief, and deep lines scoring the flesh on either side. And that is how he will look when he finds out who told. He might be back at any moment. How did she think she would live with him after this. It is not possible. And if he should be arrested? She sees a policeman's face carved in professional disinterest. "Mr. Pearsey? I have to advise you that under section 49 . . ." But the private screening of what might be switches without warning to what was and the policeman's face is looking at her, or at least at a point just above her head, and saying "Come on now, stand back," while her own eyes are fixed and cannot stop looking at the face against the step.

Noreen's brother in the chilly light pours luke-warm tea and gulps it down abstractedly. Noreen, too jaunty with determination, comes downstairs and into the kitchen to make toast. Her knife clatters on the plate but she will not allow it to unsettle her.

"Cold out," she says, at once regretting.

"Where've you bin?" says her brother, with whom conversation has always been a game of onesies up against a brick wall, with random strays lobbed back only now and then from the other side. In fact her brother has no desire at all to know, is thinking only of his father and why he is not back and whether the bastards took him after all, though he said it was safe as a church. But Noreen panics.

"I went to call Nolan, if you must know," she says, sure

now that he must have seen. So that now he is indeed alerted.

"What do you want with that creep?"

"Nothin you'd be interested in."

Their mother, coming in in her dressing gown, putting the milk away, does not see Noreen run her tongue across her top lip. Nor does she hear, as she fills the kettle, her son hiss, "Dirty slut."

The officer who received the message from the switchboard read it through again, wanting to find a use for it. It hadn't come in till five-thirty. He'd had both men in custody for more than half an hour by then. Still, he thought. Still. Shake things up a bit. See what falls out. It never did any harm.

He went back into the first room.

The man there, the younger of the two, sat with his chin jutting out, inviting. Hit me you bastard and I'll see you never work again. But the officer was past wanting to hit people.

It took him a long time, the man being taciturn, not ready to play, but he worked at the words and prodded them along and tilted them in the right direction until they clicked into formation and said what he wanted the man to hear; it was someone local who blew the whistle. The man's chin jutted higher.

After a decent interval, during which he considered the accuracy of his guess and juggled words again but only for effect, the officer got up to go. He paused at the door. "Give your lawyer's name to the constable," he said. "If you need one."

The man in the other room, the older man, sat patiently and simply. He wore no expression, was neither resentful, nor defiant, and was certainly not scared. His fingers had rolled the foil from his cigarettes into a ball and he pushed it around the surface of the table while the officer talked. He was saying nothing. He knew this was no interrogation. Here was something coming at him, an ugly dog sidling up.

"It's got to be too easy. Hasn't it?" the officer was saying. "Either you're setting us up while you go for something bigger," or, he pushed the ashtray across, "you're being set up."

Here it came, whatever it was.

"Well, you knew it was a phone call—?"

Now the placid man's skin was all alive, his nerves like ants running under the surface.

"Oh, yes. Came in early this morning. Didn't leave a name. Funnily enough. But we know the area."

"Yeah," said the quiet man, to sound sarcastic, on fire with wanting to know.

"And it was a woman's voice. Or a girl's. But of course your own domestic relations are entirely scrupulous. Wouldn't you say?"

The man could not control his upper lip. Strings of muscle drew it up on one side. God, he could kill the bastard and shut his mouth forever.

But the officer was getting up from where he had propped himself on the edge of the table. He picked up the ball of silver paper and flicked it with his thumb into the waste bin. "Have your statement ready," he said as he went out.

The man sat unmoved. He would forget what he had been told. It would be lies.

As he went back down the corridor, the officer glanced in at the first man. He sat awkwardly, his hand wandering repeatedly to the hair at the back if his head, his neck rising and turning in his collar like a bird's.

The officer was pleased. Something could still come of it. You never knew.

Noreen's brother is seated on the floral sofa in front of the TV with his spoiled leg resting on a red velour cushion with fringes. He is so stuffed with anger that he feels his skin must split. The ones who told him are waiting to see what he will do. It will kill his father, he knows it. The anger creeps in a slow burn up his neck, floods his jaw purple.

Her own father. Her own family. He might have been there himself. Would have. He does not know how she found out. They have come to him for that. Their faces a blank wall while they wait to see what he will do. He cannot imagine how she knew so much, or when.

Quickly, his mouth open as if to speak, he sits up and leans forward, resting his arms on his knees, one hand gripping the other. He is careful not to look at the others. Remembering. Her quick feet on the stairs. She was out of breath, the blood in her racing. Her hand shook, he heard the knife on the plate. And her face. Her face, the bitch. Jesus Christ, he could murder her with his own two hands and not be sorry. The bitch, the bloody bitch.

"Well, you'll have to see to her," he says. "And her fella."

The plainclothes man cruising in his Honda is getting bored. This is his third day. He must pay careful attention to register everything he sees, not knowing when the least significant event will become the thing they have been waiting for and explode with a shower of useful names and faces.

Down the road a white van comes round the corner too fast. At the same time the plainclothes man realizes he is opposite the club again, the one his department would like to shut down. He pulls over.

Noreen on the floor of the van is trying to keep her balance. Her hands stick to the metal. Her eyes are closed, her mouth is closed against the tar. It scorches her lungs. She would close her nostrils if she could. They have tarred her head, her face, her hands, and they have daubed it on her clothes. Someone slit a pillow and pushed her face into the feathers. The tar burns her lips, the membrane of her nose, the rim of an eyelid; it burns her finger ends where she has chewed them. She keeps her eyes closed when the van stops, does not open them even when the hands take hold of her, bundling her out with her head down as if she were the evening's arrest, caught on a news clip.

The plainclothes man sees the driver and two other men hustle something forward between them. Something like a figure but bent and with a wildness he cannot quite make out about the head. He radios his chief. On no account must he lose the men.

Inside the club, Noreen crouches in a pool of coloured light in the centre of the dance floor where they have pushed her. The woman who screamed briefly when they bumped her table has stopped as suddenly. Noreen does not move. Her nose is streaming to quench the burn. She has not opened her eyes.

She does not know where they have brought her, nor what will happen next. She senses only the light and the blank faces of the men and women watching, whom it would not surprise at all should she prove to be the entertainment.

The three men, loose particles in the wake of the shock, run out of the club.

In the small space of his hesitation the plainclothes man sees Noreen, ungainly in the spotlight, trying to get up. She begins to unfold, her body twisting, rising off-centre with its elbows angled up and out like wings, her head bowed under its bizarre headress, from which pieces detach and float in the coloured light. She could be about to enter a dance of great and primal beauty.

The people at the front look away. At the back they pick up their drinks again. The plainclothes man heads for his car.

BURNING BRIGHT

AT SEVENTEEN MINUTES TO FOUR ON THE AFTERNOON OF Sunday July 3rd, Deidre Justhrope-Fielding, age thirty-one, a resident of West Heights, sunbathing on her freshly stained cedar deck, opened her eyes abruptly at the touch of twin jets of hot, musk air on her upper lip, and stared full in the yellow eyes of the cougar.

Of the two pads of cologne that dropped from her waking eyes, one landed and lodged precariously on her left breast. A distraction she chose to ignore. It seemed wise in the circumstances to keep all movement to a minimum, to move perhaps not at all. Ms. Deidre Justhrope-Fielding made up her mind not even to blink.

The cougar appeared to have the same resolve.

Or perhaps a cougar has no eyelids. Ms. Justhrope-Fielding looked hard at the great feline head lamps.

Brass-coloured glass. Marbles. Resting in black rubber rings that were fine like skin. Wet rubber. Washers sunk in the fur.

No eyelids.

The cougar appeared to have a distinct advantage over Deidre.

The muscles of her temples and forehead squealed to let go and send her own eyelids slamming down to squeeze this unthinkable apparition, the other eyes, out of her vision like pips from a lemon.

She resisted the impulse. The twin jets came again, stronger this time and the hairs on her own upper lip, the fuzz that she had always wished would bleach out or, preferably, disappear, stood up of their own accord and shivered in the hot airstream. Heavy with the smoke of charred bark, musk, the breath below burned and scented—and stopped. Deidre watched the flat nose and the two commas of the nostrils. The rims of the commas contracted, diminishing the diameter of the holes by a skin's thickness, no more, then flared with a motion like the wings of a ray and contracted again. Drawing in, drawing in.

Deidre watched, taking care not to blink, as the holes closed; and although she had not communicated with any living non-human thing—had been careful not to since callous childhood, when she had kept a glandular-smelling tortoise in a shoe-box only to have it die there disgustingly—she knew, nevertheless, without a whiff of doubt, that this animal was smelling her. Mesmerized, she watched—yes it can be said that she witnessed—her own smell disappearing through the commas, sucked irretrievably into the twin tunnels that led straight to the brain of the cat.

So long did she watch—as long as it took the commas to become mere exclamation marks—that she no longer knew what the great luminous brass marbles were doing. To glance up now might well bring the whole confrontation to a precipitate finale. Caution. Caution at all costs. Even a Girl Guide—though Deidre had never been attracted to the Guides, preferring the promised glamour of ballet classes, until her thighs grew too thick—even a Girl Guide would know that much.

Holding fast to this invaluable piece of forest lore, Deidre let her eyes gradually, so very gradually, leave the exclamation marks and begin to travel over the delicate, rubbery membrane at the tip of the cat's nose and then slowly, with painstaking care, continue hair by hair over the short, cut-velvet pile of its broad bridge and so back up towards the yellow eyes.

It was here that she had considerable difficulty disregarding her own nose, which intruded whitely into her vision, being furred, though less obviously than her lip with fine hairs, a down so fine that it had not at all taxed her tolerance until this moment when it lifted with an electricity all its own.

Nor was her throat quite right.

The whole of her neck seemed to have swollen to such enormous girth that it could hardly be said to be a neck at all. There seemed to be both an inward and an outward distension so that had Deidre been capable of expelling the air that she had bagged in her lungs she might have heard only a shrill whistle, for all the passage that remained in the centre was a mere thread-like tube. It was in this tubule that the word "Alex!" had lodged.

The word had bubbled there as soon as the cat's image had registered on her sun-blasted retinas, a micro-moment, no more, before a single, concussive thump also registered, like a slammed door in a far back room of her brain.

But Alex was still spinning home in what Deidre called his nasty little Nippon number, listening to KIKM and giving not a thought either to Deidre or to the towering, spruce-spiked granite beside the road, but, rather, rehearsing with both care and conviction his explanation of last week's sales figures to the Tuesday breakfast meeting.

To call or want to call Alex, however, was an understandable impulse in Deidre, who was in the habit of relinquishing her tenuous hold on independence the moment she heard his car putter to a stop at her front door. "Aa-lex!' with its two falling notes intoned in the minor key of the foghorn was a familiar prelude to any one of a number of requests: perhaps a capricious call to open the wine, or a more heavily fraught summons to fetch her towel from the hook. No request too small—and some more urgent than others.

That Deidre overlooked his absence at this particular moment of waking might, in the circumstances, be forgiven her. It was not the recollection of his absence that stoppered his name permanently in her constricted throat but, rather, that deeply ingrained knowledge of the need for caution.

And so her eyes continued, hair by tawny hair, over the face while her mind registered a new sound in the reverberations of the thud. It was barely detectable and yet it was unmistakable: a sigh, a long-drawn aspirate, nothing more yet, the wind on a leaf. And if her eyes had not been focused so narrowly, intent upon their calculated upward progress, Ms. Justhrope-Fielding might have detected also a new movement to accompany the sound: a rising, slow and subtle but unmistakable, of the whiskers beside the animal's nose and immediately below her highly concentrated field of vision, a rising caused by the bunching of the skin and fur there as the flesh over the upper jaw drew slowly back.

As her eyes surfaced again into the yellow glare of the cougar, the soughing wind became a chafing, rasping blast, rusted metal dragged across ice, iron bars singing in forty below.

Ms. Deidre Justhrope-Fielding looked deep into the eyes of the cat. And the eyes were burning. Bright. Not with warmth but with a cold, naphthous flare that matched the exhalation of its breath, coming now fast like snow sliding from a roof.

The rush of sound seemed to tear at her own lungs, seemed to boil through her own veins and arteries in an almighty embolism and thunder round inside her head like a blood beat, a birth storm, a death rattle. It was not comfortable.

To escape this torrent of sound, she sought the soundless depths of the eyes and through the narrow slits of the pupils she let herself be drawn down into the still, dark pool at the centre of the blaze. Here the fire raged in silence and fed upon itself eternally, a black hole consuming whole constellations of light, sucking them in noiselessly through the narrow slits, eating its own corona.

Deidre Justhrope-Fielding had found, though she had never thought once in her life to look for it, the absolute. Here was an infinity of innocence, the beauty of eternity. Ms. Deidre Justhrope-Fielding simply had to close her eyes.

About the Artist

Born and raised in Birtle, Manitoba, Kerri Andrews moved to Winnipeg eight years ago to find her fame and fortune. She has recently graduated from the Advertising Art Program at Red River College and hopes to stay in Winnipeg to continue to explore other creative avenues.

Recent Turnstone Titles

Days and Nights on the Amazon
   A novel by Darlene Barry Quaife

Accountable Advances
   Short fiction by Dave Williamson

Hearts Wild
   Short stories edited by Wayne Tefs

This Business with Elijah
   Interrelated stories by Sheldon Oberman

Sitting Opposite My Brother
   Short fiction by David Bergen
   Winner of the John Hirsch Award for Most Promising Manitoba Writer